The Tree

Tales from a Revolution: New-Hampshire

The Tree

Lars D. H. Hedbor

Brief Candle
Press

Cover and book design: Brief Candle Press.
Cover image based on "Irvington Woods," Albert Bierstadt.
Map reproduction courtesy of Library of Congress, Geography and Map Division.
Fonts: Allegheney, Doves Type, and IM FELL English.

First Brief Candle Press edition published 2019.
www.briefcandlepress.com

ISBN: 978-1-942319-35-1

Dedication

to Sharri,
and all the other
readers who make this
work worthwhile

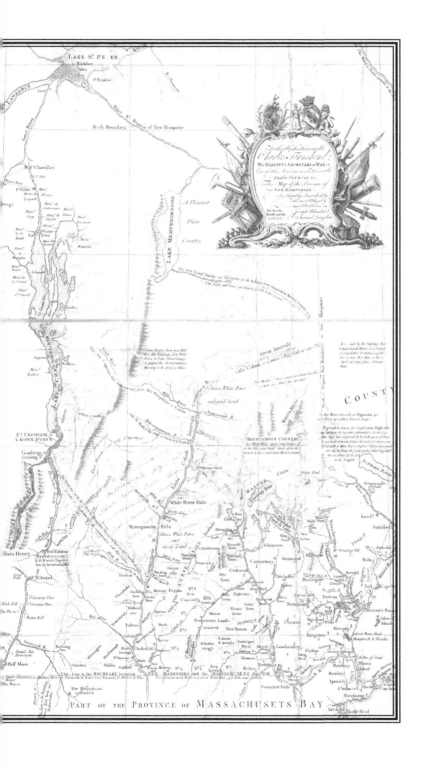

Chapter I

Abimeal Sawyer crouched alongside the creek, scowling. He knew that he had to get water for the house, and all the way out to the creek, he'd been crunching through frozen grass, his frown deepening with every step, anticipating the sight he now beheld.

It had been cold enough overnight to freeze the slow-moving creek, and now he had to clear ice from the surface before he could dip out enough for his father's morning tea and their gruel. He missed his mother's cooking almost more than anything else, though of course he would never say that aloud.

He'd had to fill in where he could for the work she did around the house, while his father threw himself into his work with more fury than he had even through the long months of his mother's final descent into weakness and death. At least she could rest in the little graveyard just beyond the boundaries of the village.

As for those she left behind, there was always more work to do. With a resigned shake of his head, Abe crouched and used the bowl of the old dipper to crack the ice. He tossed the shattered bits out onto the ground, watching them settle and begin melting as he waited for the mud to clear from the hole he'd made in the surface of the stream.

When the water again ran clear, he lifted one dipper full after another up to fill the wooden pail. Its worn and loosened sides seeped some of the water right back out again, but he knew from experience that once he had it filled up past the top band, he'd be able to get enough water back to the house to fill the kettle and stir into the pot with a precious handful of meal.

Nearly every day started the same way, and by the time he got back, he knew that his father would be grumbling about how long it had taken him and chiding him to hurry, always hurry, so that the day of work could begin in earnest.

Despite their family name, Abe's father worked not as a sawyer, but as a lumber cutter, selecting and felling the trees that were then sawn into boards and sent over to England for building the fine houses and warehouses of London and beyond.

Cyrus Sawyer had managed only a few years past to persuade a surveyor to come out to his grant to mark which trees had to be kept for the King's Navy, and which he could cut without further limitation. Having gotten that boon, he had set himself the task of extracting every shilling he could from the grant, and this focus had driven him to only hire assistance when he could not otherwise get the work done, while working himself ragged day after day.

Abe remembered the grim set of his father's mouth when his mother had started coughing harder and harder with each passing day, taking longer to get her work at the hearth done, and having to pause frequently as she labored for breath. The day that she had brought a handkerchief away from her mouth after a particularly prolonged fit, and Abe and his father had seen it stained scarlet with blood, his father had said only, "Mind you help your mam, boy, and do as she bids you."

The first morning that she had been too weak to rise from her bed, Abe's father had pushed the dipper and bucket into the boy's hands. "You know what needs doing."

And when his mother had coughed her last, her rattling breath falling silent and her skin waxen and cold, his father had grimaced outright, reaching for his cash-purse and measuring out the coins to hand to Abe. "Go and fetch the pastor, and bid him hire the grave-digger."

Abe had slipped out, unwilling to let his father see the hot tears that threatened. The last he saw of his mother, his father was bending over her corpse, closing her sightless eyes with uncharacteristic gentleness. The pastor's wife had kept Abe in her warm, bustling kitchen while her husband attended to the necessary tasks for a burial. The loaf she'd offered him, fresh from the fine bread-oven alongside her hearth, should have been ambrosia, but it tasted like ashes in Abe's mouth.

The winding-sheet had seemed to Abe like too little to shield her from the soil that the gravedigger began shoveling into the grave after the pastor had finished with his part of the ceremony. The clods fell with a muffled sound, and Abe looked away, willing himself to think of something—anything—else.

He'd noted a raven standing upon one of the gravestones, crooking its head at him and uttering a low croak of a call. The bird seemed to be looking at him almost in sympathy, but Abe knew that it was beyond the simple creature's ken to understand the pain and loss that he was feeling.

Later, Abe had fled the house and his father's unyielding silence, seeking instead the comfort of the woods. He walked at first, and then broke into a run, his feet finding their way along the familiar paths without conscious effort on his part. The part of the family grant that his father had already worked fell behind, and he slowed as he entered the virgin forest where his childhood footpaths had become overgrown and tangled.

He had stopped finally in a small clearing where he had spent many a quiet afternoon in his younger days. Surrounded by soaring pine trees, it felt more like a sacred place to him than did the village's small church, and certainly more comforting than the graveyard would ever be again.

He'd leaned his back against one of the great pine's trunks and slid down to sit on the soft ground. This tree, like all of those around the clearing, was marked with three hatchet slashes into the bark, forming the King's broad arrow. Abe's father had explained to him that this signified that it was reserved to use as a mast for one of the Navy's great sailing-ships, chosen for its size and apparent soundness.

It had struck Abe as odd to consider that these seemingly unmovable boles might someday travel the globe under the Crown's broad pennant, but for now they formed a firm, solid, comforting cage for his wild and uncontrolled thoughts.

What could possibly drive his father to strive for riches even as his wife lay dying? What kind of world was it where a mother could be parted from her child by rough cloth and mounded earth? How would Abe find his way into a future without her, and with only a rare glance from his father?

The dim light of the forest had darkened into evening before Abe rose from the ground and made his way back to the house. There, his father was scraping something burned and blackened out of the spider, his habitual frown deepened into an outright scowl. "Supper's ruined," he'd said, and jerked his head to the small barrel beside the hearth. "Have an apple."

Abe had nodded and taken one of the last of the hoarded fruits. He'd retreated to his pallet in the corner and bitten thoughtfully into the apple, chewing slowly and trying to ignore the redness he'd glimpsed around his father's eyes, a hint that the man might be anything but as emotionless as a stone.

Chapter 2

The kettle was steaming and the meal had softened enough to eat before Abe's father spoke. "Working out at the edge of the big clearing today. You'd best stay clear. Plenty to do here."

"Yes, sir," Abe said, hiding his irritation. While he had no desire to work on his father's crew, he didn't like being treated as though he was his father's housewife, responsible for all of the household chores in his mother's absence.

He spooned out his serving of gruel and sat down at the heavy table to eat. The pail sat beside the hearth, leaking the last of the hard-won water out onto the floor. He'd have to clean the mess that left, in addition to the rest of the ordinary daily work.

Slurping at his gruel, he looked over at the sack that held the dried beef he'd bought a fortnight prior. While he knew that his father would scowl at the extravagance, he decided to make a stew with it for supper. There were a few onions left, and he thought he might even be able to shake a bit of flour out of the cask to thicken it. It would be nice, though, to have a few other staples.

It was too cold to bathe in the creek, and he was just as glad for that. He ran his fingers through his hair, thinking that it might be time to cut it again. Or, he thought, he could just keep his hat on his head when he was out in public and let it go a bit longer.

"Might I have some money for eggs?" His old aunt—his

father's sister—kept an unruly flock of chickens in town, and had offered him a handsome price the last time he'd passed by. He thought he might be able to get her to go even lower, if he sweet-talked her enough. Like her brother, though, she was usually taciturn and dour, so it was hard to predict.

His father grunted, "What for?"

"Thought they'd be a nice break from the gruel. The meal's mostly gone anyway, so I should get some more soon, and flour besides." Abe marveled at his boldness, even as he cringed inwardly in expectation of his father's inevitable explosion.

Instead, his father sighed. "I suppose. You ain't getting any smaller. Got to eat; soon I'll start showing you the trade, need your strength for that." He passed over a handful of coins.

"Tell my sister hello for me."

Abe took the money, saying, "Yes, sir." He didn't think that the old woman would much care whether he conveyed his father's greetings or not, but he also knew that there was every chance that if he failed to do so, his father would learn of it somehow, and that would be just yet another failure for which he could be berated.

Cyrus Sawyer stood from the table, slurping down the last of his tea, and dashing the dregs into the fire, where they hissed and popped. He set the cup down on the table, swept his shaggy hair back, and slipped his work hat firmly over his head.

"Mind yourself in town, son," he said, pausing briefly at the door to look at Abe. Already taking his father's cup from the table to wash it, Abe nodded and didn't even look up until after the door had swung closed with a bang.

He finished tidying up, deciding that the water by the hearth would dry by itself. He banked the fire and donned his hat and jacket, picking up the pail and dipper again. The air had warmed as the sun climbed the sky, and birdsong along the track toward the village made it seem almost more like springtime than the early days of autumn.

The first hint of fall's riotous colors on the hills around the house, though, revealed the season too clearly for any mere birds' singing to overcome. He returned to the stream and dipped out enough water to soak the beef in, shaking his head at the degree to which the ice had already melted away from the edges of the hole he'd made.

Pouring the water into the raised spider and setting it over the banked fire to just warm it, he pulled out the dried beef and dropped it in. Satisfied, he swung his rucksack over his shoulder and went back out into the bright sunshine and started for the village. He jingled the money in his coin purse and wished that he could afford some squash, but that was a battle for another day. Today, he would get just the flour, meal, and eggs, and he knew that his father's flinty figuring would leave him no money for any other luxuries.

He decided to go first to the mercantile for the meal and flour. No sense in chancing the fragile eggs to more travel than was strictly necessary, and he knew, too, that there was always a chance that his aunt would be in a rare talkative mood, and he wanted to be sure that he wasn't held up so long that Mister Harper at the mercantile was already gone for the afternoon.

On the porch at Harper's, there was one of the usual pairs of bored old men, perusing the same old broadsides from down in Boston or Philadelphia, and arguing over their content. As Abe came within earshot, he could hear that the perennial topic was

Governor Wentworth's unwelcome energy of late in regard to surveying and inspecting lumber. He stopped just within earshot, interested in hearing the inevitable argument.

"Those accursed surveyors little Johnny has been sending around to lay a measuring rod on every plank and log have been threatening to put the mark on any lumber they like," one old man said, spitting onto the street for emphasis.

"Nay, not just any," said another, holding his hands up in a placating gesture. "The timber or boards must be plainly in violation of the King's Mark."

His interlocutor spat again. "And once the mark is set upon the lumber, the sheriff seizes it up, and the owner of the sawmill must pay whatever fine he cares to assess, else say farewell to their lumber and their profits, easy as kiss your hand." He lifted the back of his hand to his lips and tossed it by way of demonstration.

Again the other man shook his head. "Now, Ephram, you know that ain't true. The fines are assessed according to the law, which states what fine should be laid on what size timber, all orderly and reasonable-like."

Ephram grumbled, "All I can say is that I liked Governor Wentworth's uncle better, when he were Governor over this colony. He was a right reasonable fellow and tended to his own affairs. Up here in the woods, I like swamp law better'n any mast law, and it troubles me to hear you argue against that, Amos."

"Have a care, Ephram. If we push the governor too far, it will give the Parliament cause to tighten the screws even further."

"Let them try," Ephram exploded. "What good is it to grant a man a parcel of land, and then deny him the blessings of that soil?"

"'Tis but a condition of that grant," Amos said calmly.

"That condition should be set upon the grant, not changed at a whim later. And when we must beg for the surveyor's deputy to find the time to come and tell us what we may and may not use from our own land, while fallen timber rots and is wasted, I suppose that you call that but a condition as well?"

Ephram scowled at the other man, glaring at him until Amos finally shook his head and said, "We are here at the sufferance of the King and Parliament. If you like a grant that you may do with as you please, why not prove out a nice farm instead? I'm sure that you could get Governor Wentworth to make you a nice offer, given enough of an inducement."

Ephram said nothing in reply, but only spat a third time, rounding on Abe. "You, there. Your pap, he works that grant of his and has to leave whole stands of trees be, even when experience shows that no more than one out of every twenty will ever be fit for the King's purposes. How does he like that?"

Abe was startled and alarmed to be drawn into the argument. "Well, uh, to be honest, he hasn't said, at least not anywhere that I could hear him."

"Aye, well that one don't say much where anyone can hear him. You got business with Harper, then?"

"Yes, sir," Abe said, walking around the two men. He thought he saw Amos giving him a sympathetic look as he passed.

The merchant was glad enough to see him, though he didn't seem in much of a mood to dicker over prices. In the end, though, Abe was able to purchase the flour he wanted, and even a little more meal than he had anticipated. Perhaps he could make somewhat bigger servings of gruel than usual, and his father would be well enough satisfied that Abe had made a good bargain.

By the time he came out, his rucksack bulging with the supplies he'd purchased, the old men were much more amicably discussing the shortcomings of Governor Clinton over in New-York. On that question they apparently had no significant disagreement.

The sun had risen high into the sky, and he was feeling warmed through for the first time since he'd left the kitchen that morning. The songbirds were still out in force, calling back and forth to one another, telling stories of love and desire, possession and warning.

One tree in particular seemed laden down with their tiny bodies, the noise almost deafening as Abe passed underneath. He skirted around the outer boundary of the canopy, not wishing to become as decorated as the ground under it was.

From the other side of the road, he felt a chill come over him as he heard the deep croaking call of the raven. As he spotted the fell bird sitting on the branch of a tree there, he almost wished that he had chanced the songbirds instead. The black-feathered creature regarded him as he passed, its head cocking from side to side.

When Abe had passed by without acknowledging the raven, it hopped into the air and perched on the next tree along his route, again uttering a hoarse croak at him. Abe glared at it now, and while he couldn't be sure that it was the same animal that had been present in the graveyard when his mother had been laid to rest, something made him feel certain that it was.

The creature's repeated calls and bobbing head seemed almost provocative to him, daring him to respond. He stooped and picked up a pebble to toss at the unwelcome creature. The bird clearly understood what his intention was and flapped away, calling out disapprovingly as it went. Abe let the pebble drop back to the road and continued, shaking his head at the creature's antics.

The rest of the walk to his aunt's house was without incident at least, and he was soon walking through the crowd of chickens that stood like guards before the gate to the house. He knew from experience that there was no point in trying to avoid the birds—they would get out of his way on their own as he walked through the flock.

These birds, at least, threatened neither his hat nor his calm, and he was at his aunt's door without delay. As he raised his hand to rap at the door, it flew open, and his aunt stood there, weeping openly, and Abe just stood there dumbfounded at the sight.

She gathered him into her arms, sobbing so hard that he could scarcely understand her. "Oh, you poor boy. You poor, poor lad. I don't know how we're going to make it all work, but I will do what I can for you."

Abe pulled away, bewildered. "Aunt Rosanna, what are you talking about? All I need is some eggs for my father's breakfast tomorrow."

She wailed aloud and dragged him back into a damp embrace. When she could speak somewhat coherently again, she said, "Oh, my poor Abimeal, you don't know yet, do you? Your father was struck down by a falling tree, and died instantly. You are an orphan, and will be in my care from this day forward."

Chapter 3

The rucksack slipped off Abe's shoulder again as he ran, and he impatiently swung it around to hug it to his chest. The bright sunlight of the day had given way completely to night, and even the moon seemed to be in hiding, refusing to light his path home.

His feet knew the road well though, and he could find his way by only the slightest glimmer of light emitted by the broken eggs as they leaked out of the rucksack and over his fingers. He could hear the hoarse laughter of the raven that flew, unseen, behind him in the darkness.

He had to hurry, had to get home before supper time, get the stew cooking for his father, and make it good and strong, so that it would halt the tree that he could see in the distance menacing Cyrus from above, suspended over the man in a battle between gravity and willpower.

Abe gasped as he suddenly tripped on an invisible obstacle, falling into darkness, darkness without end, darkness that would swallow him whole—and then he sat up, the morning light streaming through the window of his aunt's house, sweat pouring down his face. There would be no stew, and the tree had not paused in its downward path to seal his father's fate.

Instead, today would bring another visit to the graveyard, and a fresh grave beside the still-raw scar in the earth where his mother lay. His aunt had made all of the arrangements, pressing a coin into the pastor's hand and speaking in a low voice. Abe had been spared the long, jolting wagon ride back from the clearing with his father's corpse, and could settle into the numb role of a spectator at yet another burial.

His aunt had brought him back to his father's house that same afternoon, though. "Abe, child, do you know where your father kept his savings?"

"No, ma'am, I do not. He only ever gave me shopping money and the like from his coin-purse, and that he kept on his belt at all times."

She'd pursed her lips. "Confound that man," she'd said under her breath, but Abe had heard her clearly.

Just then, the chief of the logging crew his father had employed had come to the door, and she'd slipped outside to speak with him. Abe overheard only snatches of the conversation—the man seemed more concerned about whether Aunt Rosanna was going to hold him responsible than anything else—but, to be honest, he wasn't listening.

Instead, he'd stared into the cold hearth, the banked coals under the spider long since dead and still. The meat he'd put in to soak was floating, dry and dark where it broke the surface of the water. He heard Aunt Rosanna's voice drop, as though she were asking the crew chief something in confidence, but he could not make out her words.

"No, ma'am, we never seen him do nothing like that," the man's voice was clear and penetrating in the quiet and dark of the house. "Now, about them logs we've already got felled..."

His aunt had cursed and dismissed the man then, and had

come back inside to fetch Abe. "Gather what you want from here," she'd said, her tone crisp. "You likely won't be coming back. I've a second bed you can use, and there's no sense in either of us spending more time here than we have to."

Abe had gathered his few meager belongings, stuffing them into his rucksack. Some clothes and bedding, a spare pair of shoes, and a basket his mother had woven for him to use in gathering mushrooms; everything else his eyes fell upon belonged to his father, and had always been forbidden to him.

A sense of propriety would not let him leave the meat in the spider to rot, nor the water to rust the heavy iron implement. He carried it outside, and was lugging it out to the waste pile when Aunt Rosanna snapped at him, "Just leave it, boy. I've plenty of cooking pots."

He'd swallowed hard and protested, "Just let me tip it out and dry it, ma'am? The water will ruin the spider if I don't."

Her mouth had tightened into a thin, cold line, but she nodded. "Do what you must, Abe. We leave in a trice, though, so as to be back to town before dark." He'd returned the spider, empty, to the hearth, and had wiped it down, but he knew from experience that the lack of a fire to warm and dry it thoroughly would likely mean a layer of rust within days. He hoped that the grease from the meat would be enough to protect the surface, even as he'd known that it didn't matter.

Since they'd gotten back to the village, though, she had been almost solicitous toward him. Now, as he lay down into the unfamiliar raised bed, he could see a dying branch of the tree outside the window, the few leaves that remained on it already dulled to brown. It seemed as though everything vital and living was departing from the world in this season of decay, and he wished for a moment that there were some way to stop the ravages of time.

The room was warmer than he was accustomed to. Being at the top of the steep, narrow stairs was part of it, he knew, but his aunt also kept the hearth well supplied. She had little tolerance for the chill, it seemed, and he was just going to have to get used to it.

He was going to need to adjust to a lot of things. He heard Aunt Rosanna moving around downstairs, a splash of water and the sound of logs being stirred about on the grate. She called upstairs, "I heard you shout, boy. Is all aright?"

"Yes, ma'am," he called back, adding, "I had a bad dream, is all."

He could almost hear her curt nod. "Aye, I shouldn't be surprised at all if you have them for a while yet. Come on down, then, and let us have some eggs to break our fast."

The thought of eggs gave him a pang of sadness, as he realized that they would no longer be a meal for a special indulgence, but were simply the most economical food she had to offer. He climbed out of the bed and pulled his trousers on over his long shirt.

"Jakes are out back, if you need them," she said, with a jerk of her chin. "Just had them cleaned out this spring, and it's cold yet this morning, so the smell ain't too bad."

He nodded his gratitude and slipped out the door. When he came back, she was stirring eggs in a cup, and the smoky, salty smell of rashers of bacon filled the air, their bubble and pop a welcome music. He had known that his aunt lived somewhat better than his father chose to, but he never expected this level of opulence.

"Made enough for us both today. After this, you can cook when you rise. I'll show you how to care for the chickens, too, so you can help out around here, earn your keep. Do you take tea?"

"No, ma'am," he said, startled. His father had never offered him tea, as he'd felt that it was a drink for adults only. It was an oddly appealing thought that one result of his sudden change in circumstances was that he would be given responsibilities other than housework. The removal of the looming prospect of joining his father at the handle of an axe was a terribly mixed blessing.

Aunt Rosanna lifted the bacon out of the pan onto a pair of plates with a long-handled fork and tipped the grease into the fire, where it flared up, smoking and spitting. She poured the eggs into the pan and stirred them. Abe could feel his mouth watering at the prospect of such a rich meal, and for a moment he forgot the sadness that awaited him in the day to come.

"Your father and I grew up in this house, you know." As she turned the eggs to cook them through, his aunt spoke over her shoulder. "We had to share that bed that you have to yourself, until he was apprenticed out as a woodcutter."

She flipped the egg onto one plate, cutting it in half and pushing Abe's portion onto another plate with his bacon. "When he got his land grant, after your grandfather died, he gave his part in the house to me, since he didn't have any further use for it."

She shrugged, handing Abe his plate. "I never figured on having to share the house, but I couldn't bring myself to get rid of the old bed, so there we are. Eat, eat. There's no need to wait for an old woman to stop nattering on when there's food getting cold."

She motioned him over to the table and sat. She shook her head slowly, looking at the stairs to the bedroom overhead. "Never thought I'd be burying my little brother. He always had the big plans, all the ambition, wanted to make enough money to buy a place back in England, even talked about getting into politics and changing how things were done."

She sighed. "Now, the money's gone, my brother's gone, and all that's left is the grant . . . and you."

She turned to regard Abe. "Of course, we'll have to talk about what's to be done with the grant. Best use of it is to just keep selling the timber, but my brother was terribly careful about doing everything on the safe side of the law."

She nodded, more to herself than to Abe. "Made sense, what with him wanting to go into politics some day. It was one of the few times I saw him give up the possibility of turning up an extra shilling, but it were always with the long view in mind."

She fixed Abe with a flinty stare. "The long view didn't get him very far, so I think we'll put our faith into what brings in the best money while we're still alive to enjoy it." She chuckled to herself, and started shoveling the eggs up to her mouth with a crisp rasher of bacon.

Abe shook himself from the uneasy stillness he'd adopted while his aunt spoke, and followed suit, but the appeal of the food had waned.

Chapter 4

Like a repeating nightmare, Abe found himself standing beside a mound of soil again, listening to the first clods of dirt falling onto a lifeless body at the bottom of the grave. His aunt stood with him instead of his father this time, but otherwise everything else seemed the same. He even wondered whether they had wrapped Cyrus in the same winding cloth somehow.

He looked around at the gravestones again and was almost surprised that the raven wasn't there to jeer at him. Instead, there were only the silent graven words and embellishments on the stones that stood all about, silent testimony to the inevitability of the fate of all men.

Aunt Rosanna pulled at his arm, and he realized that the pastor and other mourners—none paid, all business associates or even friends of the dead man—were all departing the graveyard to let the gravedigger complete his work in solitude.

He followed, his steps reluctant. Reluctant not to leave, as others might suppose, but reluctant to go. What was there to go toward? He'd had a future, even if not one of his own choosing, but without his father to apprentice to, what remained of that? He could hardly apprentice to the crew who had worked for his father.

His aunt could readily enough provide him a bed and all the eggs he could eat, but there was more to life than just that. He was just coming to the dour conclusion that his aunt was hardly likely to let him sit idly about the house anyway when he saw something that stopped him in his tracks.

There, standing by the road where the group of mourners were passing, was the figure of a girl facing away from him, dressed normally enough, her hair tucked neatly up into her mob cap, unremarkable in every way but one. On her shoulder stood a raven—and Abe felt certain that it was the same bird that had tormented him—and moreover, she appeared to be holding an animated conversation with it.

While he couldn't make out her words, he could see her gesturing as she spoke, and the raven bobbing up and down on her shoulder as it croaked in what looked for all the world like a deliberate answer

Pulled irresistibly by the spectacle that nobody else in the procession seemed to have taken note of, Abe approached the girl. "Pardon me, miss, but is this your raven?"

She turned, and he could see the laughter in her eyes, and noticed that peeking out of the side of her mob cap was a sprig of some dried, brown plant. "Nay, but I am his person, 'Tis true enough."

He raised an eyebrow at her. "And what does he call his person, if I may be so bold as to ask?"

She laughed outright now. "Most days, just 'Craw.'"

He laughed with her, the sound of his own laughter strange in his ears. Just then, Aunt Rosanna noticed that he had stopped, and called out to him, a harsh tone in her voice. "Keep up with us, boy, and do not think to tarry with that girl."

For some reason, this made Craw—Abe thought that he

might as well call her that in his mind, at least until he could learn her real name—laugh again. She made a dismissive gesture with a wave of her fingertips. "Go, go! Your aunt is right, you should not be seen in my company."

She leaned toward him and added in a conspiratorial whisper, "She is about to tell you all about my witchcraft and sorcerous ways, but perhaps I will tell you the truth when next we meet by chance."

She turned away again, and Abe hurried to rejoin his aunt, her glare giving his feet all the encouragement they needed. When he reached her side, she reached out and seized his elbow, almost hard enough to make him cry out.

She hissed at him, "You keep your distance from Miss Randall, do you hear me? She is touched, and there are those who say that she consorts with the Devil himself." She turned her glare to the girl, who was walking away, sharing some confidence with the bird on her shoulder.

His aunt sniffed, adding, "'Tis enough that she has made a pet of that accursed bird. When she sends it around to spy upon the house, it disturbs the chickens and disrupts their laying."

Abe crooked an eyebrow at his aunt in disbelief, but kept his counsel, certain that she would not receive well any skepticism of her claim that the girl was using the raven as a spy. His aunt did not notice, muttering almost more to herself than to Abe, "'Tis fortunate for her that witches are no longer burnt or put to the question, as they were in Massachusetts-Bay, back in the days of your forebears."

Something in the way that she said it made Abe think that she didn't entirely disapprove of this old-fashioned approach to dealing with strange women whose ways she didn't understand. Of course, he thought with a wry smile to himself, she was strange enough herself that it was probably just as fortunate for her that the old ways had passed with the coming of the modern world.

She had already moved on to other thoughts, though, and he heard her grumbling under her breath, "I'll never understand how my brother could have accumulated such a large funeral party, without he has left the money to feed them, never mind to pay the pastor and the gravedigger . . . " She trailed off, still grumbling under her breath.

When the funeral party arrived at her house, their number had dwindled significantly, and no more than a handful of men remained. His father's crew chief, a couple of members of the crew, and men who Abe had seen around town, but whose business with his father he didn't know all followed Rosanna as she shooed chickens out of the path up to her porch.

"Come on in, then," she said, standing on the porch and holding open the door. The men filed past her, looking askance at the chickens that milled around at their feet.

A plate of pickled eggs, somehow stained a rich brown, and some apples from the fall harvest on another plate, were the extent of the offerings Aunt Rosanna had set out for her guests. Abe could see the men exchanging glances, but none of them said anything aloud about her stinginess.

She entered behind them and pulled the door firmly closed behind her. Abe imagined that it was to keep the hens, who knew that it was past feeding time, from invading the house in search of their cracked corn. She turned around to face the men and clapped her hands, feigning delight at seeing them there.

"All right boys, help yourself to some food. Can I get any of you some switchel, or perhaps some cider? I haven't a lot, since my poor brother's took the secret of where he secured his fortune to the grave with him today, but I'm happy to share what I have with you." The lie seemed likely to cause her face to crack outright, but nobody believed her enough to take her up on it.

One man said only, "I wouldn't think to impose on you, Miss Sawyer. I'm just glad to gather with Cyrus' friends and remember the man."

The others nodded and several murmured, "Hear, hear."

The crew chief revealed a bottle he'd had in his rucksack, though, and said, "Never fear, Miss Rosanna. I brought a little something to toast his memory, if you can but supply the cups."

This met with general approval, and Aunt Rosanna nodded to Abe curtly. "There are some cups in the sideboard opposite the hearth. Go and fetch them, and mind that they're clean."

Abe said, quickly, "Yes, ma'am," and hurried off to find the cups. In the kitchen, he saw an open shelf with some cookware on it along one wall, but on the wall opposite the hearth, there was a cabinet with three stout-looking doors. He opened the first, hoping that it was the sideboard that she'd mentioned.

He saw no cups within, but he did see a leather bag behind a couple of stacked saucepans. He reached around the pans to feel the bag and see whether there were any cups behind it, but when his hand touched it, it clinked heavily, as though it were filled with coins.

Overcome with curiosity, he moved the saucepans out of the way, placing them on top of the cabinet, and pulled the bag out into the light. He untied the top of it, and was shocked to see a jumble of heavy gold coins within, the dour face of King George gazing back at him from the depths of the bag.

He heard a noise from the other room that sounded as though his aunt might be coming in to check on him, and quickly re-closed the bag, shoving it back into the cabinet. He closed the first door, his heart pounding, and opened the second, where he found a motley collection of tin cups.

He glanced toward the doorway, but nobody was there, so he gathered up the cups, peering into the depths of each to be sure that it had been put away in a usable state of cleanliness, and carried the lot of them into the other room, hoping that his shaking hands would not betray him as he handed them out.

Aunt Rosanna was engaged in a curt conversation with one of the businessmen and looked up at Abe just long enough to see that he had the cups before returning to her discussion. The crew chief, though, said quietly, "Thank you, boy. You should have some with the rest of us—after all, Mister Sawyer was your father."

Abe held out one of the cups to receive a short pour of the brown liquor the man was sharing about, and earned a short bark of laughter when, without waiting for the toast to his father's memory, he tossed it back. As he gasped and choked at the burning route the liquor traced down his throat to continued chortles from the crew chief, he thought that at least it gave him something other than the mystery of his aunt's apparent riches to think about.

Chapter 5

"**B**oy, are you awake up there?" Aunt Rosanna's bellow up the stairs jerked Abe out of a deep sleep. "Daylight's wasting, and there are things to be done. Come along, show a leg!"

At least this morning, there had been no nightmare, although Abe felt a little bit as though he'd awoken into one. His father beneath the cold earth beside his mother, his decidedly odd and mysterious aunt now responsible for him, everything that was familiar and comfortable ripped away in an instant.

Downstairs, his aunt was already briskly stirring up the eggs for their breakfast, and had set out two mugs of thin tea, this time without asking whether he wanted it. He shrugged inwardly, not wanting to appear ungrateful. Looking outside as he picked up his tea, Abe noted with surprise that there was a heavy frost on the window, though it was still as warm as summer in the house.

Of course, a woman with a sack full of money in the cupboard could readily afford the profligate use of firewood necessary to keep her house balmy year-round, Abe reflected, but he was accustomed by long habit to carefully bank the fire at the end of the day—and to accept that the morning chores were the best way to warm up after waking.

Not that it appeared that Aunt Roseanna had any intention of letting him get a chill today. As soon as their plates were clear, she led him about the house, showing him how to do for himself, and what needed doing for her and the chickens.

"The cock crows just before sunrise, unless there's some disturbance in the night, or he's just feeling cantankerous, in which case he'll crow any old time he likes. Come morning, all the chickens get corn and any kitchen scraps there might be. Mid-day, once the ice on the well has had a chance to be broken through by someone else in the village, I'll fetch them their water, and some for us, along with them."

She peered down her nose at him. "Your father had told me that you took up the cooking after your mother died. Is that true?"

"Yes, ma'am, most of it, though I have no particular gift for it."

"You may have noticed already that my gifts in that regard are sadly limited. I've always cooked very plain, and could stand to have some variety on my table. I'll have you take care of cooking supper, unless you have other chores at the time to occupy you."

She nodded, the matter settled in her mind. "Before supper, we'll gather up what eggs the hens have given us. They usually lay in just a couple of spots, which I'll show you, but sometimes they decide to get clever and lay a clutch of eggs somewhere else. That happens, we have to learn whether the eggs are still good when we find them."

She rolled her eyes, and Abe had to repress a chuckle. The thought of the chickens outsmarting her was somehow highly entertaining. "Put them in a bowl of water, and if they float, we dispose of them. If they're not rotten, we can cook them up and feed them to back to the chickens, but it's not easy to tell when an egg is rotten, so I don't often chance it."

She wrinkled up her nose. "You find just one egg that's gone fully around the bend, and it's enough for a lifetime." This time Abe did laugh aloud, and she gave him a tolerant but brief smile.

She pointed to a barrel in the corner of the kitchen. "Since we're coming into the winter season, the chickens won't lay as much until spring. Some have already slowed down, because of their molt. We need to put eggs away for the winter, and they go in that barrel. Once there are enough to make a layer, we'll cover them with the slaked lime I keep in the pitcher beside it. Preserves them all through the winter, so it's worth the expense."

Abe peered inside, and could see that the barrel was already half-full, the eggs just visible through the milky liquid. "Does that really work?"

She fixed him with an expression of feigned indignation. "I can sell those eggs right through the winter, and none is ever the wiser that they were not laid that very day." She frowned. "Not that I conceal from my customers that they are put up from the fall, but I don't borrow trouble by shouting it in the village square."

She opened the back door and went outside, beckoning him to follow. "I sell eggs to all comers at the same price, without favor toward any. Threepence per dozen, with a ha'pence discount for specie. Most buy in specie, and I like money that clinks better than money that folds; the latter is too easy to forge, and the former spends just as well after a year as it did when you earned it."

He thought to himself that this philosophy might explain the existence of the bag of hard currency in the kitchen, though it failed to provide a reason for what had looked like a very large amount of specie.

She made a dismissive gesture with her hand. "In any event, I will not ask you to handle the money. Should someone's wife appear while I am out with an empty basket, let her have what she wants, and leave me to collect from her or her husband myself. Mind that you keep good records of the transaction. You can write, can you not?"

"Uh . . . no, ma'am, my mother wanted to send me to school to learn my letters, but my father forbade it, as he said that it would not serve me as a woodcutter."

Aunt Rosanna's mouth pursed in an expression of deep disapproval. She shook her head, her tone exasperated. "That man. I loved my brother, as much as anyone could, but there were times when he would spend a pound to save a shilling."

Abe looked at her, unsure. "Does that mean that you're going to send me to school?"

She snapped brusquely, "Certainly not. I'll teach you myself. I've nothing better to do most afternoons, and I thought for many years about opening a school myself, as I do not much approve of the way that Mister Andrews conducts his classes."

Abe had no idea what she might be talking about. "Do you mean to say that he teaches improperly, or encourages free thinking?"

"Nay, nothing so bold as that, else the people of the village would have run him off years ago. No, he is merely too tolerant of misbehavior in his classroom, whereas I prefer a teacher who spares not the rod, nor risks spoiling the child."

Abe swallowed hard. His father had delivered him a thrashing just a few times, and it was an experience that he was not eager to relive at Rosanna's hands. Just then, they heard someone hallooing from the front of the house.

Aunt Rosanna waved him back into the house. "Attend
ıe closely, but say nothing, lest you confuse a business transaction.
'hat sounds like Harper from the mercantile. He doesn't often sell
ıy eggs for me, but he might be interested in a barrel of them that
've got put up from earlier this summer."

She shot Abe a wry look over her shoulder as she bustled
ırough the house to the front door. "For some reason, there are
eople in this town who prefer not to dicker with me if they can do
 at the mercantile instead."

Still chuckling, she opened the door. Harper was there, but
ɔ was Miss Randall, this time without the raven on her shoulder.
'he chuckle died in her throat and she asked, crisply, "What business
ave you here with this girl?"

Harper gave her an ingratiating smile. "As you know, Miss
awyer, Betty here keeps goats up at the west end of the village, and
ıe came to me looking to sell a goat in order to buy some chickens,
ɔ that she can keep a couple at her place. I don't have any chickens,
f course, but I offered to bring her to you and see what I could to
ɔ facilitate the exchange."

Rosanna ignored the man, jerking her chin at the girl and
ıying, crisply. "How many chickens do you look to get for a goat,
ɪd how much meat will the goat give?"

Betty inclined her head respectfully, and Abe could again see
 sprig of something brown and leafy tucked into her cap behind her
ır. "Yes, miss. Four chickens seem fair to me, and a goat will yield
ıough to feed the two of you for most of a fortnight, more if you
re frugal with the meat. Or you could salt it and have it through the
'inter. I could help with that, if you like."

Aunt Rosanna sniffed. "I know well enough how to salt

meat, as I've been doing it since before you were a gleam in you
mother's eye. Three laying hens, and the goat had better be
yearling, not some stringy old billy."

"Aye, miss, I will ensure it. Shall I go and bring it?"

"Do so," Rosanna said dismissing the girl with a wave o
her hand.

She turned to the merchant. "Mister Harper, I am sur
that you hoped to be compensated for acting as middleman to th
agreement between us. As you could see, we needed nobody t
broker a deal, but because I appreciate you bringing Miss Randall t
me, I'll be happy to let you have a barrel of limed eggs at a handsom
price."

The merchant grinned widely. "Always one to make
sharp deal, aren't you?" He sighed and looked up at the heaven
as he concentrated for a moment. "Eight bob for a cask of thirt
dozen?"

Aunt Rosanna scowled deeply, correcting him. "The cas
holds thirty-eight dozens, and I'll take no less than two crowns fo
the lot of them."

"Nine and three," the merchant fired back, his expressio
one of delight.

"Done, sir."

"Done, madam. I ought to have fetched both my purs
and cart before coming to visit with you. I shall return with bot
shortly."

Abe's head whirled as he tried to figure whether Aun
Rosanna had gotten the better of either deal, but after she closed th
door, the look of grim satisfaction on her face told him that it woul
be a rare day when she did not profit in her dealings.

Chapter 6

After the shop keeper had come and retrieved the barrel of preserved eggs from Aunt Rosanna's cellar—"You might have mentioned that I should have brought a boy to help carry them up!"—she sat at the kitchen table and chuckled to herself at the image of him puffing and straining to roll the barrel up out of the cellar and out to his cart.

For his part, Abe didn't think it was nearly as funny, particularly since he'd been enlisted to help the man, and ensure that the barrel didn't roll back down. The rope and pulley system at the top of the stairs for the purpose helped, but it was still heavy work, and he'd gotten his fingers pinched more than once in the process. The sweat that had sprung to his brow as he'd worked had quickly become icy on his skin in the crisp autumn air.

Fortunately, his fingers didn't seem to be hurt too badly, and her habit of keeping the house balmy had quickly eliminated his chill, but he still didn't share his aunt's mirth. He was happy, though, to take a moment's rest in the kitchen with her as they waited for Miss Randall to arrive with the goat for the second transaction of the day.

"Have you slaughtered an animal before, boy?"

"Nay, what meat I've had has always been salted, except for when someone gifted us with something fresh from their own larder."

"Well, I don't mean to keep the beast alive a moment longer than I must, so I'll show you how it's done this afternoon, and we'll have some of it for supper tonight and breakfast tomorrow. The rest I'll put up in salt for later in the year."

"Aye, ma'am," Abe said, and wearily folded his arms and rested his head on them.

"Ha! You think you're tired now, boy, you'll soon be really tired." Aunt Rosanna cackled and rose from the table. "We didn't fetch water, what with all the excitement. You rest up here, and I'll get it today, but tomorrow, I expect you to do it without being told."

"Yes, ma'am," Abe mumbled. After the door closed behind her, he felt tears spring into his eyes. His father was never hesitant about asking him to take on the chores that had to be done, but he had not laughed about the hardships he imposed on others, either. And his mother—he choked back a sob at the memory of the sound of soil falling on her winding cloth—his mother would never have permitted him to be worked like a servant by his aunt.

He wished that the cathedral of mast trees was nearby, and that he could retreat to their peaceful, quiet company for a while. No chore had seemed too daunting in the face of those soaring trunks, whose growth had been the work of decades of rain and soil. No trial had seemed to measure up to the storms that those huge creations had weathered.

Without the comfort of that copse of trees at hand, all that was left to him was grief and tears, though, and he permitted himself the luxury of a few minutes of both. His tears had soaked through the cloth of his sleeve, and in his old kitchen would have made his arm cold.

He sat bolt upright as he heard a knock at the door and the goatherd's voice chiding the animal, "Quiet, Miss Molly. I can't bring you back to your mama, no."

He wiped the tears from his face as well as he could, and stood to open the door. There, Miss Randall stood with her goat secured by a short rope. The raven was back on her shoulder, and at this close range, Abe could swear that the creature was looking right through him into his soul, so concentrated was its attention to him.

For her part, Miss Randall looked a bit unsure of herself as she took note of Abe's appearance. "Have I come at a bad time?"

Before Abe could answer her question, she nodded sagely and answered herself. "Of course I have. There is no such thing as a good time to come calling on someone who has recently lost both his parents."

She tilted her head, and the raven mimicked her motion—or was it the other way around?—saying, "You have my sympathies, friend. I also lost my parents, though that was three whole years ago, and I had to make my own way, instead of having family to take me in."

Abe opened his mouth to reply—although he could think of nothing appropriate to say—when the girl reached out and put her hand on his shoulder, leaning toward him and saying quietly, after a pointed look around to ensure that his aunt was not within earshot, "Though, perhaps, I was the lucky one in that regard."

Leaning back and returning to the proper distance between them, she said, more loudly, "In any event, I have brought the goat, as agreed with your aunt. Is she about, so that we can select the hens I am to receive?"

Regaining his power of speech at last, Abe said, "Nay, she is getting water, but should be along soon. Should you like to come inside to wait? You can tie the goat to the tree there, if you like."

She considered for a moment, and then nodded. "Miss Molly wouldn't normally wander, but she is missing her mama and the rest of the herd. I picked her because she's the fattest of the kids from this spring, and I wanted to be sure that your aunt would be satisfied with the tenderness of the meat, whenever she gets around to eating it."

"You . . . name your goats?" Abe swallowed hard. He didn't have the heart to tell the girl that 'Miss Molly' was destined for the chopping block that very evening.

"But of course," she said, and giggled. "How else am I to tell them what to do? I can't very well say, 'Ho there, you with the black saddle, stop eating Mister Blackwood's pear tree,' now can I? But if I call out, 'Victor, stop that now,' well, he knows I'm speaking to him, and he stops."

She frowned to herself. "Well, not Victor, because he's headstrong and very, very hungry, but you take my meaning."

Abe did not, but he didn't think it polite to say so.

"In any event, give me a moment to tie up Miss Molly, and then we can go inside."

"Certainly, Miss Randall." Abe pulled the door mostly closed behind him, mindful of how much warmth was rushing out around him.

As she stooped to tie up the goat, the girl turned and addressed the raven on her shoulder. "Did you hear what he called me? 'Miss Randall' indeed. I told him that you call me Craw, and he's already forgotten."

"Craw," the raven agreed, turning to look back at Abe, who was thinking that it might not be so wise to be in a closed-up room with the girl and her bird. He couldn't decide which was stranger—that the bird would choose to keep her company, or that she spoke to the creature and seemed to carry on conversations with it.

Finished securing the goat, which immediately started bleating and straining at the rope, she stood and said brightly, "Shall we go inside, then?"

The knot she'd tied must have been poorly-made, or else the goat more determined than she'd expected, for it broke loose almost as soon as she stood up. Instead of making for home, though, it rushed past her and straight to the doorway, shouldering Abe out of the way to get in.

The girl shrieked, "Miss Molly, no! You naughty goat, get back here at once!" She gathered her skirts up and marched toward Abe, her expression fierce. The raven spread its wings and launched itself into the air at her outburst, coming to land on a branch where it could watch the scene from above.

For his part, Abe was staring in shocked horror as the animal burst back out of the kitchen, where it had done a quick lap around the table, and ran back toward him, clearly planning to break past him through the door a second time. Without thinking, he stepped back into the house and slammed the door to stop it, only realizing after the girl pounded on it from the outside that he had shut it right in her face.

"Just a moment, Craw, let me see if I can get hold of your goat." Miss Molly had come to a skidding stop and was panting and looking at Abe with desperation. He noticed that the animal's eyes looked like some drawing of a demon's eyes, and his aunt's words came back to him.

"Miss Molly won't come to anyone but me. Let me in to deal with her." The goat, true to the girl's prediction, did not respond well to Abe trying to reach a hand out to it, and skittered back into motion, running into the kitchen again. Abe could readily see that the animal would be impossible for him to catch alone, and he opened the door a crack.

"Come in, hurry. She's in the kitchen." The girl slipped into the door, and he closed it firmly behind her again.

"Miss Molly, you come here right this moment." The goat, which had frozen in the corner of the kitchen, launched back into motion at the sound of her voice, and got past her to run up the stairs to Abe's room. Abe was horrified to see how nimbly the animal mounted the steep stairs, and he hurried to follow and chase it back down.

He got no more than three steps up, though, before the animal came rushing back down the stairs at top speed, knocking Abe to the floor, where he lay gasping, the breath knocked out of him for a moment. The goat continued its rampage, heading back toward the kitchen.

The girl, calling out over her shoulder, "Are you okay?" rushed toward the kitchen door. As Miss Molly shot past her, she was able to seize the rope trailing behind the beast, bringing the goat up short.

The struggling animal fell to the floor, bleating piteously, its legs still churning furiously in the air. The front door opened, and Aunt Rosanna walked in, carrying two heavy buckets of water. She took in the scene at a glance, closed the door firmly behind herself, and said, with a stern frown on her face, "Why on earth are you playing with our dinner, and why are you doing it inside my house?"

Abe opened his mouth to explain the absurd scene, but no words came to him. The goat scrambled back to its feet and hid itself behind Miss Randall's skirts, almost as though it had understood what its fate was to be.

Unwinding the rope from about her ankles, the girl held it out to Aunt Rosanna, her tone one of quiet dignity. "Your goat, ma'am, as we agreed. She took fright when Abe answered the door and got inside."

Aunt Rosanna's mouth formed a harsh, tight line for a moment, and then she snatched the rope from the girl's hand. "I'd have thought that you could have used your ways to better control the animal."

Miss Randall started to reply, but Aunt Rosanna interrupted her. "You've delivered on your part of our bargain. I need nothing further from you. Abe knows which birds to deliver up to you." She indicated the front door with a tilt of her head, her mouth still pursed disapprovingly, and the girl gave a little gasp and ran out, the door banging shut onto its latch behind her.

Aunt Rosanna turned to Abe then, and said tartly, "Don't tarry. Give her the chickens and get back inside."

Abe said sullenly, "If you needed to bawl someone out, you should have yelled at me. It was my fault that the goat got inside, after all."

Aunt Rosanna's nostrils flared, but she said only, "And you'll be cleaning up any mess the creature left behind, too. In the meantime, you'll do best to keep your mind to yourself in my business dealings."

Chapter 7

The less Abe thought about the fate of poor Miss Molly, the happier he was. First had come the accusing look from Craw, who clearly was not anticipating that her goat was so soon slated for the table. After she left with the hens Aunt Rosanna had picked out for her, then came the awful moment when his aunt actually dispatched the goat.

The rest of the process had been no less horrifying. Although he had been frustrated at the elusive animal as it tore through the house, that frustration did not extend to wanting to see its demise. With the smell of a simple stew spreading through the house, though, he was finding it somewhat easier to forget about all of that, and focus more on the meal to come.

For her part, Aunt Rosanna was still scowling through the entire process, particularly when she found droppings the animal had left in the kitchen. While she worked on putting up the meat in salt, as promised, she'd made Abe clean up the mess, tsking to herself over the scratches in the floorboards the creature's desperate scrambles through the house had left.

When he was done, she returned to instructing him in the process of putting the meat up. "I would rather do this in the summertime, when I could put the meat out to dry in the sun after the salt's drawn the water out of it, but then, this way there is less chance for the chickens to get into it."

She was cutting the meat into thin slices, leaving as little as possible on the bones and laying the meat onto a layer of salt she had scattered out across a flat board. The bones she tossed into her biggest kettle—"That will make a broth that we can turn into some good soups."—and when the board was covered in meat slices, she sprinkled a generous layer of salt over it.

"We'll leave this to give up water for a day or two, and then set it on racks to dry out the rest of the way. After that, we'll pack it in fresh salt in a barrel and put it in the cellar. You know what to do with the salted meat, so let's get the stock going."

Here, Abe felt on more solid ground. "Have you onions and sage?"

"Of course," his aunt replied. "Do you take me for a savage, or worse, a Virginian?" Her sharp tone was belied by a sly smile at the edge of her mouth, though. "Onions are in the cellar, in the bin just behind the door. Sage is hanging from the rafter toward the front of the house. You'll know it when you smell it."

She dismissed him through the kitchen door with a jerk of her chin. The evening was gathering, the light fading earlier each day as the autumn slipped away toward winter, and the cellar was gloomy and close. However, the onions were easy enough to see in the light that still filtered down through the door, and though there were many bundles of herbs hanging to dry in the darkest part of the cellar, he was able to locate the sage by feel and smell readily enough.

He brought a couple of onions and a few leaves of sage up to the kitchen, and his aunt nodded approvingly. "Knife's just there. Trim up the onions as you see fit, and then we'll go and get some water for the stock while there's still a little light."

She handed him a pair of wooden buckets, and he noticed that their seams were freshly caulked in pine pitch. No hurrying to use the water before it leaked out here, he thought, with a pang of homesickness that surprised him. How many times had he cursed that leaky old bucket of his father's?

Lost in thought, he didn't notice his aunt stiffen as they approached the village well. He did notice, however, her crisp tone. "A fair evening to you, Missus Martin," she said, everything but her words clearly conveying that she wished the woman something quite a bit less than a fair evening.

"Why, if it isn't Chickie Sawyer," the other woman answered. "Still no rooster for you, though I hear that you've picked up a little orphaned chick of your own?"

"Aye," Aunt Rosanna said, her voice even, though Abe could tell that she was holding back a fury that would break a lesser woman. "Abimeal here is my late brother's son, but we're only here for some water, not for gossip from a tart tongue."

"As am I, as am I," the woman said smoothly, unperturbed by the barb Aunt Rosanna had thrown her way. She paused theatrically before asking Abe, "What does she feed you, dear? Eggs breakfast, lunch, and supper, I dare say?"

"I've no complaints about the food my aunt provides, ma'am," Abe said, uncomfortable to find that he felt moved to defend Rosanna against this noxious woman. He added, "It happens that even while my father lived, we bought eggs from her for our own table, as we liked them for a fortifying meal, as often as we could."

The woman smiled thinly. "So sad for you, Rosanna, to have lost a paying customer, as well as a brother. Why between that and having to feed another mouth, I worry for your domestic felicity, with no rooster to call your own."

Aunt Rosanna cocked her head at the woman and regarded her for a moment, the gesture reminding Abe forcefully of Craw and her raven. "My domestic felicity is in better shape than is that of someone whose rooster, as you put it, is out crowing out of windows all over town."

The other woman colored deeply, her eyes turning cold and angry. "My Jacob roosts at home, thank you very much, and you'll do well to keep your nasty rumor-mongering to yourself." For some reason, Abe felt persuaded by her reaction that his aunt's comment had hit home. In any case, Missus Martin was apparently done with her business at the well, as she turned and left without so much as a good evening to aunt and nephew.

When she had bustled out of sight, Aunt Rosanna visibly slumped, and Abe was surprised to see that her hands shook as she reached for the rope to pull water up from the well.

Abe ventured, "She is an unpleasant woman, if you'll pardon me speaking ill of my elders."

His aunt uttered a sharp bark of laughter. "Aye, that she is, and no need to apologize for speaking ill of such as her. She has plagued me since we were girls and I got something that she wanted very much for herself. She didn't care to work hard enough to earn it for herself but wanted only to take it from me."

Seeing Abe's look of curiosity, she said primly, "We'll speak no further of it. The light's nearly gone, and we have water to fetch." She drew up the first bucket full of water and poured it carefully into her own, then handed the rope to Abe.

By the time all of their buckets were filled, Abe's arms ached from the unfamiliar motion of lifting water up from under the ground, and he was glad enough to carry it to the relative comfort and warmth of his aunt's house, where the stew was hot and ready. Dinner was a quiet, thoughtful affair.

As he drifted off to sleep, he thought he caught a snatch of sound that might have been—unlikely as it seemed—a woman's sob from the first floor of the warm, dark house. He shook his head, dismissing it as impossible to even imagine.

Chapter 8

It had been a fortnight since everything had changed, and although he'd had no more nightmares, waking in the suffocating heat of the upstairs bedroom was no less a shock than it had been that first morning. Some mornings, Abe lay abed for a while, just remembering his parents, and wondering why Providence had put him on such a difficult road.

Other mornings were like this one, when Aunt Rosanna awoke before he did, and called upstairs impatiently, "Shake those bones, boy! Work to do today."

Abe sighed and slid upright, his feet getting tangled for a moment in the blanket he'd tossed over the side of his bed in the night. What manner of work awaited today he did not know, but he had already learned that his aunt was not one to tolerate idle hands that were capable of doing something productive.

He'd not seen Craw again since she had hurriedly left with her chickens, but he had encountered her raven a couple of times around town. He understood better his aunt's dark comments about the bird spying on her, when he had awakened one morning to find it peering through the window into his room, turning its head this way and that as it regarded him.

When the raven had seen him looking back, it had spread its wings slowly—even, had Abe believed that a bird were capable of such a thing, insolently. While still eyeing him, the raven had dropped off the branch outside the window, flying back toward the hills behind the village without vocal comment.

Abe untangled his feet and dressed quickly, knowing that his aunt would be as impatient as she usually was in the morning. When he descended the stairs and entered the kitchen, he found the customary mug of tea waiting for him, and eggs that his aunt had somehow contrived to turn green as she cooked them.

He yearned for another morning of the stew, or even the broth from the goat, but inwardly shrugged, chiding himself for looking askance at his good fortune. He took a bite, suspicious, but they tasted normal, so he went ahead and ate them with his normal healthy appetite. He slurped at his tea, having grown accustomed to the bitter, somehow drying beverage, and looked expectantly at his aunt as she sat and cleared her throat.

"We'll be going out to your father's grant today," she said, without preamble. "Need to look over the work that the woodcutter's crew has gotten done already and discuss what's to be done next." She grimaced, and Abe realized that this was going to mean visiting the scene of his father's demise.

The tea suddenly tasted like burnt charcoal in his mouth, and he pushed the half-drunk mug away, his appetite ruined. He asked, trying to keep the despair he felt out of his voice, "Can't you go alone?"

"Nay, not only would it look most improper for an unaccompanied woman to meet with a group of men, but there may be legal agreements which must be concluded." She looked slightly uncomfortable as she mentioned this last point, and Abe's curiosity was immediately raised.

"What do you mean?"

Aunt Rosanna seemed to choose her words carefully, and she said, delicately, "I am not empowered at this time to make decisions about your father's estate, and there has been no time to record a change in ownership with the sheriff, even if I were in such a position."

"I do not follow your meaning. What change in ownership?" Abe felt a rising sense of panic, though he knew not where it came from.

Aunt Rosanna's hands fluttered above the table and she said, "A dead man cannot hold a grant from the governor, of course. You are not yet of legal age—"

"I will be, soon enough," Abe interjected, but his aunt continued as though he'd said nothing.

"—and as your father died intestate, that leaves the question of inheritance unclear. If he had written a will with you as his heir, and me as his executor, I could readily enough manage the affairs of the estate on your behalf."

Abe's jaw dropped as he came to understand what she was saying. "Do you mean to say that I am the legal owner of my father's land grant?"

"Aye, before the law, but as a practical matter, I will manage the grant in your best interest. In the meantime, should there be any matters of formal contracts, I need you with me today to make your mark, so that they may bind the woodcutter crew."

Abe thought furiously, then asked, "And what nature of contract are you contemplating?"

Aunt Rosanna said diffidently, "I have been but speaking with the crew about what area of the grant should be cut next, as we exhaust the current lot."

Something about his aunt's reply seemed evasive, but Abe had to tell himself to stop being so suspicious. After all, Aunt Rosanna was blood, and hadn't she willingly made room for him in a life that was clearly full enough for her purposes already? As he thought about it, he realized that making wise decisions about the stewardship of the land grant required experience and knowledge that was well beyond his ken. He ought to be grateful that she was willing to take this burden on as well.

He nodded and said, "Aye, that makes sense. I was only hoping to avoid the very spot where my father fell, if that might be possible."

"Of course," his aunt said smoothly, and the suspicious voice in the back of his head noted that she appeared to be relieved that he was no longer questioning her about the issue.

His curiosity forced him to ask, though, "Can you tell me what lot you have talked with the crew about working next?"

She gave him a look through narrowed eyes and nodded slowly. "Certainly. I forget that you probably know those woods nearly as well as did your father."

Better in some ways, Abe thought to himself, but did not say anything aloud.

She continued, "They had pretty well finished the lot nearest the road when your father had his accident. They have now cleared it, save for the trees bearing the King's mark, of course."

She spread her hands across the table. "So the road is here"—she drew a line along one edge of the area she'd covered—"and there's an area that is a bit swampy over here." She indicated an area further along the road with a wave of her fingers.

"If they fell the trees in that area over the winter, while the

ound is hard and any open water is covered in good ice, we can
oid wasting that part of the grant." She frowned. "The crew
ief is arguing that even with the ground frozen solid, working in
at part of the grant is too risky, and he's suggesting a different lot
work on through the winter."

Abe nodded in agreement. "But pretty well all of the rest of
e grant can be worked any time of the year. If we're to log that
t at all, it has to be in the winter, I agree. Of course, the trees there
e not as sound as elsewhere on the grant, and I think my father
d planned to leave it unworked, at least for now."

"That may be, but the road being hard by that lot is another
ctor. They can move the trees they fell more easily from there than
ey can from further into the grant, particularly in winter."

Abe frowned, thinking. "The first snow has yet to fly, and if
ey're already finished with the current lot, they'll need something
do while we wait for the ice to firm up enough to be reasonably
fe to work on. Can they not simply push further up the hill on the
r side of where they are?"

"Aye, they can, but they will need to work around a number
mast trees along the edge of the lot. I suspect that your father
ew the lines where he did because those trees are in the way. He
ely hoped that the royal surveyor would come and take those at
me point soon, clearing the way to work back from the road."

She pursed her lips and gazed out the window. "Of course,
ere's another possibility, too. If we simply look the other way
hile the crew takes the mast trees and delivers them to the mill,
e can have them out of the way, and also realize a tidy profit."

Alarmed, Abe asked, "Won't the mills know that we are
nding them illegal timber and report it to the sheriff?"

She gave him a knowing smile. "Nay, for they can sell th lumber they cut from it at a high price as well, and I know for a fac that many of the mills in this area are happy enough to get the hands on trunks that are suspiciously straight and long."

She grinned. "They always have demand for large dimensio lumber, and even if they are caught red-handed, everyone know that they need pay their fines and the King's surveyor will releas the logs without any further fuss."

With a hoarse laugh, she added, "Of course it used to b better—back in the day, so long as the shipyards were getting wha they wanted, old Benning Wentworth didn't give two shakes how many mast trees we used ourselves. The new Governor Wentworth-Benning's nephew—decided that there was money to be made fo the Crown and set out to enforce the pine tree laws, never mind tha we can still supply more masts than all of Portsmouth can use."

"What happens if one simply refuses to pay the fine?"

Aunt Rosanna chuckled. "Well, that would make for a ver interesting day indeed, now wouldn't it? I imagine that the sherit would swear out a warrant for your arrest, and you would get th opportunity to see how living in a gaol compares to living wit me."

Chapter 9

Standing amidst the stumps that had occupied his father's last days, Abe thought it somehow fitting that a cold rain should start falling. Aunt Rosanna had read the weather signs well, though, and they were both dressed warmly, with cloaks that would stand the wet—for a while.

She'd left him standing by himself while she engaged in furious, sometimes shouted, negotiations with the woodcutter crew where they were paused in their work. While she gestured wildly in the direction of the swamp, Abe started off in the direction of the lot in question. It had been some time since he'd seen it, and he was curious about the actual conditions there.

The steely clouds continued to spit icy rain, occasional drops of which found their way under the broad brim of his hat, where they further chilled his skin. The wind shifted, and he could hear the woodcutter's chief clearly for a moment.

"Can you even enter into binding contracts, with no will, and the boy not yet of age? Or are we all just wasting our time here?" Abe thought it a reasonable question and was eager to hear how his aunt might answer it.

Aunt Rosanna's reply was lost to the wind, though. Whatever she said, the woodcutter turned his head and spat in disgust, and Abe was surprised in spite of himself at the man's crude behavior. Shaking his head, he slipped into the scrubby woods where the ground became softer.

Completely unlike the soaring pines of his wooded cathedral, these trees were less exuberant and more determined in their growth. Their shade was somehow closer to the ground, as the lowest branches of these trees were not above the reach of a tall man, but brushing the ground.

Too, these trees did not yield to one another like gracious partners on a dance floor, but instead their branches overlapped and jostled one other, seeking light and soil from which to draw sustenance. They obviously had no trouble finding enough water, but it looked to Abe as though the overabundance of water actually held back their growth.

A little way into the woods, there was a spot where one of the trees had been toppled by a recent storm, its roots pulled out of the soft earth, leaving a rock-studded hollow where it had been. The rare break in the shadowy darkness of these woods allowed the rain to again assault Abe, and he pulled his jacket closer to conserve what warmth he had left.

There was a rustle of movement at the top of the overturned root system, and a large raven landed there, perching and turning his head in its characteristic curious motions. Abe had no doubt that this was Craw's companion, come to check up on him.

He smiled at the bird, which was by now familiar enough to be almost welcome. He wondered once again whether it was actually spying on him and reporting what it saw back to the girl, as unlikely as that seemed.

"Cold day for flying," he said to the raven. The bird blinked at him, still just turning its head from side to side, but offering no reply. Abe almost started laughing at himself for expecting the bird to reply, and for even being disappointed when it remained silent.

He felt certain that if Craw had witnessed the interaction, she would have told him to get his own bird. Or-he corrected himself on her behalf-to become the chosen pet of a different bird. This one had chosen-assuming that it was her companion at all. If it were not her bird, then it was certainly one which had no interest in adopting *him*.

With the rain threatening to turn to sleet, Abe lost interest in pursuing conversation with the raven, and shaking his head at his own silliness, he turned around and headed back toward the recently-cleared land that had claimed his father's life, wondering whether his aunt had convinced the woodcutters' chief of anything constructive.

The woods were so dense that he nearly got turned around— there were no footpaths established, and precious few animal trails to follow—but after a few false starts, he found his way out into the clearing.

Aunt Rosanna and the woodcutter were up at the side of the cleared lot that was opposite the road where the sliver of land that he had discussed with her lay. They were pacing off the length of the section together, and from that Abe concluded that they had come to a meeting of the minds, and that now they were just discussing details.

The raven appeared overhead, and circled around Abe before landing on the stump nearest to him. Abe gave it a frown, and moved toward where Aunt Rosanna and the woodcutter were. The bird trailed him, hopping and flying from stump to stump, until Abe finally turned around to face it.

"Why are you following me around?" Once again, he felt

strange talking to a bird, but the raven shifted its weight from one foot to the other now and bobbed its head up and down enthusiastically.

"Craw, craw!" The bird's raspy call was loud enough that Aunt Rosanna looked over at him sharply from the other side of the clearing. He saw her shake her head dismissively and turn back to her discussion with the woodcutter.

Abe was reasonably certain now that this was actually the girl's companion, but he still could not imagine why it was suddenly attending him. Turning back to face the animal, he said, "Well, that doesn't really answer my question. Did Craw send you to follow me around?"

The raven grew more agitated now, bobbing its head and appearing almost to shrug as it called again, "Craw, craw, craw!" Then it spread its wings and flew right at Abe, who ducked and raised his arms instinctively to protect himself.

The raven swept past, and Abe couldn't help taking note of the bird's wickedly hooked bill as it skimmed past his head. It wheeled around and came to a landing on his upraised arm, its talons gripping firmly through the thick fabric of his jacket as he froze, torn between fear and wonder. Slowly, he lowered his arm, and the bird adjusted its grip as he did so, turning its head to stare him intently in the eye.

It made a low, bubbling call, shrugging as before, and followed it with a more typical croak. Abe was still staring in wonder at the bird, suddenly realizing just how heavy it was, when he spied his aunt noticing that the raven now perched on his arm.

From across the clearing, she waved her arms, shouting just audibly, "What in the Devil are you doing? You let that bird go ight this instant!" The woodcutters forgotten, she began storming across the clearing.

The bird turned to face her, again calling, "Craw, craw!"

Abe objected, "I'm not holding it, ma'am. It landed on me s all." He held his arm up to show that the bird was there of its own accord, and it spread its wings, which Abe was amazed to see spanned almost as wide a space as his own outstretched arms might.

He thought that it would fly off then, but having shown ts size, the raven folded up its wings again and waited, seemingly content for Aunt Rosanna to come nearer. His aunt stopped a few paces away and stood there, her hands balled onto her hips, blinking cold rain out of her eyes.

She hissed at him, her eyes flashing, "Do you think to join Miss Randall in her practice of consorting with fell forces?"

"Nay, ma'am, I was but standing here, and the creature accosted me."

She raised an eyebrow at him. "Do you expect me to believe that this bird is standing on your arm of its own free will?"

"Aye, ma'am. I've done nothing to either draw it here, nor to encourage it to stay." He demonstrated by raising and lowering his arm again, and the raven again spread its wings to maintain its balance on his arm.

His aunt scowled and advanced on him, waving her arms at the bird. "Leave at once, you unnatural beast! What do you think you're doing?" A small part of Abe's mind observed with amusement that he was not the only one now speaking to the animal.

As she got nearer, the raven finally launched itself into the air, flying just barely above Aunt Rosanna's head before flying away in the direction of the village. She watched it for a moment before turning back to Abe. "While you were befriending woodland creatures and getting your shoes covered in muck, I have reached agreement with the woodcutters."

Abe nodded. "I saw you showing them the plot that we'd discussed offering to them until the swamp freezes up sufficiently."

"Aye, though they demanded a greater share than I wanted to offer them of the timber they fell for us. A full crown out of every pound paid by the mill. Why, I should feel better treated if they had merely robbed me on the road, as honest highwaymen."

Three-quarters of the money earned by their labor seemed a fair division to Abe, but he knew that he was ignorant of what was customary, so he kept his counsel.

"In any event, we'll need to write it all out, and then you'll need to make your mark, just to be sure that there is no question about whether or not they're authorized to deliver the timber up to the mill." She snorted. "At least there is no accursed stamp to pay for."

Seeing Abe's look of confusion, she said waved her hand dismissively. "It was probably before you remember, one of Parliament's addled ideas to try to extract money from the colonies. It doesn't matter, in any case. We let the Parliament know that imposing duties on us without our consent was going to cause more unrest than it was worth, and we can only hope that they don't forget it."

She looked at him with an opaque expression and added, "As to the contract, I've instructed the woodcutters to properly observe the mast trees, though it may cost some additional work. We cannot afford to have undue attention drawn to our work here while we haven't got your father's estate settled."

She was interrupted by a black shape hurtling past—the raven, flying low and fast between the two of them. She gave a cry of surprise, jumping back and falling to a seated position on the wet ground, from which she hurled invective at the bird.

Abe kept a straight face and stepped forward to offer her his hand to pull her back upright. The raven came about and glided to land on the same stump as before, where it alighted and began croaking excitedly.

As she regained her feet, Aunt Rosanna grimaced at the mud that caked the back of her dress and said, her tone exasperated, "What can that accursed bird want?"

Abe frowned thoughtfully. "It's as if it wants us to follow it somewhere."

His aunt scowled. "You had best follow it then, else it will give us no peace. I still must finish discussing the agreement with the woodcutters. Mind that you come back to the house before you catch your death from the rain."

Abe nodded as she pulled her cloak about her more tightly and turned away. He set out in the direction from which the raven had flown back toward them. The bird called out loudly and flapped into the air from the stump, flying over Abe's shoulder, then leading the way in the direction of the village.

Chapter 10

Harried from time to time by the raven, Abe hurried back toward the village. It had stopped raining, but the sky was darkening, as though it might start in earnest again at any moment. As they neared the village, the bird veered away toward the hills, and Abe followed, cutting across an open field, initially puzzled, but then with a growing conviction that the creature was leading him to Craw.

He had never been to this part of the village surroundings before, and he was struck by the tidiness of the stone fences between the fields here. He had seen fences fitted together out of the limestone that appeared as though buoyant in the soil each spring, of course, but these were laid together with exquisite care, and he took pains to avoid disturbing the rocks as he climbed over the fences.

As he clambered over the third one he encountered since leaving the road, the raven swooped around and landed on it near him. It watched him replace a stone he'd knocked askew, and hopped eagerly along the length of the fence, seeming to urge Abe on. All the while, it was uttering a low warble like the burble of a stream, punctuated by occasional croaking calls.

Once Abe had cleared the low wall, the bird was on the wing again, flying out across the field. Peering after the raven, Abe felt the first pellets of sleet hit his face, propelled by a chill wind. Huddled in a herd along the far fence of the field were a group of shaggy goats, and propped against the fence was a small, still form.

Abe ran faster than he ever thought possible, skipping from the top of one hummock to the next, cursing the uneven ground and the slick mud that threatened to send him sprawling with every step. The raven was circling the figure at the fence line, and as Abe drew near enough to confirm his fear that it was Craw who lay against the stone fence, it landed on her shoulder.

He came to a halt before her and crouched beside her, his breathing coming in great shuddering gasps. She turned her head to face Abe, a trace of a smile on her face as she said, weakly, "I knew that he could get you to come find me, but I didn't think it would take you this long."

When his breath had slowed enough to permit speech, he brushed away the sleet that was melting onto his face and asked, 'What in the name of heaven are you doing out here?"

She motioned with her eyes to the huddled goats. "I herd goats, don't you remember? This is where I herd them." She took a long breath, a sardonic smile playing across her mouth. "Normally, I would go back to the room I rent in the village during the night and in bad weather, but I fell and hurt my leg three days ago and haven't been able to walk or even crawl very far."

She reached back and patted the stones of the fence behind her. "I was able to get myself over here, though, and the goats kept crowding around me to pester for treats, so I stayed warm enough to start. Once it started raining, though, they wandered over there, and so I sent my friend off to find help." She lifted a hand into the air and the raven flapped over to perch on it.

She lowered her hand, bringing the bird back around to

tuck its head under her chin, and she nuzzled it absently. "I am afraid that I must impose upon you to carry me back down to the village, where I can probably ask my landlord for assistance."

Abe nodded. "Of course, Craw. I'll take care of you."

She started chuckling, and it grew into a belly laugh that left her wincing in pain. "Oh, Abimeal, you should hardly ever take what I say seriously. My name is Elisabeth, but my father always just called me Betty."

She was still chuckling and shaking her head fondly as he said, "Well, Betty, my mother and father always just called me Abe, and my aunt can't seem to decide whether to call me that or just 'hey, boy!'"

He smiled in response to her renewed laughter, then gestured at the miserable-looking goats. "Do we need to do anything about them before I bring you back to the village?"

"Oh, no, they are fine on their own. If I am to be laid up for any time, I may need someone to come out and check on them, but I mostly stay with them because I prefer their company to that of most people."

He gave her a wry smile. "I can't say that I blame you for that." He looked her over and frowned. "Am I to just lift you, then?"

She gave the raven a little pat and then launched it into the air from her arm where it had perched. She raised her arms toward him. "Let us try to get me standing first."

He took her hands and found them icy cold. Grimacing, he knew that the best thing he could do for her would be to get her inside to a warm place. "Which leg is hurt?"

She patted her right thigh, wincing again at the motion

He crouched beside her on that side and said, "Here," putting her arm over his shoulder. He made sure that he had a firm grip on her forearm and wrapped his other arm around her waist as he stood, pulling her upright with him.

She cried out as her right foot touched the ground, but she was able to lift it up high enough to avoid doing that again. "All right, now let's see if I can pick you up this way."

She nodded and he bent, putting his arm behind her knees and standing up, holding her in his arms. He wrinkled his nose. "I won't be able to carry you very far this way. If I put you over my shoulder, it won't be very dignified, but I'll get you back to the village faster that way. Is that all right with you?"

She smiled ruefully. "Dignity is something that I had to let go of almost three days ago. Please do what you must."

He grunted assent and set her back down onto her good foot. Coming around in front of her, he bent and placed his shoulder against her stomach and lifted her into the air, bent nearly double over his shoulder. Wrapping his arm securely around her legs, he asked, "Is this comfortable?"

She chuckled again. "No. But what other option do I have? Let us be off." He could feel her shivering against his body, and so he swung around toward the village and concentrated on carefully putting one foot in front of the other at a steady pace.

The sleet was turning to snow, the first flakes dusting the cold ground and making the footing even more treacherous. Nevertheless, in an attempt to keep Betty talking, he said over his shoulder, "Where are the chickens you got from my aunt? Do you keep them in the village, or out herding with you?"

From behind him, she answered, as though it were perfectly

ordinary to hold a conversation while travelling upside-down over someone's shoulder. "Oh, they stay in the village, though I have to pen them up to keep them from returning to your aunt's house. They lay well, and the eggs have been a welcome addition to my diet. My landlady likes them, lots better than she likes the raven."

"Well, the raven doesn't lay eggs, right?"

She chuckled for a moment, though it was obviously an effort from her position over his shoulder. "No, he doesn't, and if he were a she, the eggs would be too infrequent and too small to win anyone over."

He smiled, though he realized that she couldn't see it. "We're coming up on the first fence. I think I'm going to have to set you down on top of it, and then have you turn around to face the other way, so that I can come around the far side of the fence and pick you up again. Do you see what I plan?"

"Yes, but why don't you just use the gate?" She pointed a way down the fence, in the direction of the village, and Abe sighed.

"Because I didn't see it on the way up here." He turned at the fence line and trudged down toward the gate. "It's a good thing that I have you right here to help me find my way. You're better than your raven, though I suspect that people in town would talk even more about me if I were to routinely carry you about like this."

She laughed aloud at the thought, and he chuckled with her. "Aye," she said, "People talk enough about me with just a raven. Carrying a girl about on your shoulder to give you directions simply is not done." She delivered the last statement with a nearly perfect imitation of the prissy tone that Missus Martin employed in throwing barbs at Aunt Rosanna.

"It makes no sense to bring you to your cold room, Betty, when you need to warm up, and quickly."

"Aye," she said quietly. "But I've no place else I am welcome."

"You haven't any friends in the village you could stay with while your leg mends?" Even as he asked, he knew the answer. Why would she have sent the raven to find him, someone she barely knew, if she had friends in the village upon whom she could rely for assistance in her hour of need?

"Nay, it seems that there's a rumor about town that I am a bit peculiar, and that I am beyond the pale. Some even say that I am a witch, but we haven't had a good witch burning in these parts in a hundred years or more, so I do not concern myself with such prattle."

Abe grimaced, glad this time that she could not see his expression. His own aunt was one of those who said such things about her, he knew. Of course, Aunt Rosanna barely knew the girl, outside of business dealings with her, and the occasional encounter on the street.

With that, Abe made up his mind. "I am going to take you to my aunt's home, at least long enough to warm up. You've got a friend in the village now."

Chapter 11

The girl had fallen asleep sitting at the kitchen table, her hair escaping from under her mob cap to spread in a bedraggled fan across the tabletop. Her cheek rested on her arm, and Abe had moved another chair beside her to help her find a comfortable position for her injured leg.

He'd thrown a generous addition to the wood on the fire, for once not minding the sweltering temperature at which Aunt Rosanna liked to keep the house. Getting Craw—Betty, he corrected himself—through the door had been a delicate operation, but they'd managed, and he had set her in a chair in the kitchen as gently as he could.

It was only when he stood up from depositing her that he realized how tired he had gotten from carrying her. The snow that had started falling thickly as they regained the road into the village had left a slushy, treacherous mess on the ground, and had driven the villagers to their hearths, so he'd gotten no help in carrying her.

Of course, he'd also gotten no questions, which he supposed was a blessing. Their only company for the trip home had been the raven, which had paced them all the way back, appearing periodically out of the swirling snow to check up on them. Betty had raised her head to greet the bird a couple of times when it had appeared, but for the most part, she had fallen silent once the snow started, exhausted from her ordeal, and from the strain of being carried in such an awkward position.

At one point, Abe had become worried that she might have lapsed into unconsciousness, and he'd asked, "Betty? Are you comfortable?"

The girl had given a humorless little laugh, saying quietly, "Not comfortable, no, but grateful that we are nearly to the village . . . and very glad that you came for me." Abe had said nothing, focusing on bringing the house closer, step by step.

Now, he sat across the table from the girl and watched her sleep, her shoulders rising and falling regularly with her breath. The cloak he'd wrapped around her for warmth had slipped off one shoulder, exposing the plain, coarse cloth of her dress. He was glad to see that she was no longer shivering, and the color had returned to her cheek.

He had just laid his own head down on the table when he heard his aunt's voice outside. "Why are you spying on me again, you fell bird? Begone!"

The front door banged open then, and Aunt Rosanna called out, "Are you home, boy?" She came into the kitchen just as Betty awoke, raising her head to look up at the noise.

"Aye, ma'am." Abe looked at his aunt steadily.

Her mouth screwed up into a grimace and she said, more to herself than to them, "Well, that explains what the bird was doing here, at least."

She addressed Abe. "Now, can you explain to me why Miss Randall and her bird are here, and you without supervision with her? What manner of mischief are you engaged in with this girl, and under my roof?"

Abe shook his head sharply. "It's not like that at all, Aunt Rosanna. Miss Randall was injured in a fall, and has been exposed to the elements these past three days. She needed to warm up, and I hoped that you might know who can attend to her hurts."

His aunt looked startled for a moment, and then said briskly, "Of course. We should never hesitate to aid those in need."

"Thank you, Miss Sawyer," said Betty in a small, shaky voice.

"Certainly, child. What is the nature of your injuries?" Without waiting for an answer, she said over her shoulder to Abe, "Have you not set the kettle on to boil for some tea, at least?"

She circled the table toward the girl as Abe moved to swing the kettle, filled that morning, over the fire on its crane. Betty answered her, "It's my leg, ma'am. I don't know whether I've merely wrenched it or broken a bone."

Aunt Rosanna nodded. "Either way, we'll get you patched up. It's a fortunate thing that my boy here was able to find you and bring you to safety." She kneeled beside the girl's leg. "Abe, you should leave the room while I have a look to see what injury Miss Randall has done herself."

"Aye, ma'am." Abe went into the front room and stood by the doorway, facing away from the kitchen but within earshot.

"We probably need to get the shoe and sock off that foot first. 'Tis a good thing that you had warm socks, but you don't need them while you're here."

"Yes, ma'am." A moment later, she cried out in pain, and Abe winced sympathetically.

"All right, child, let me see if I can feel a break before I work on that any further, then."

Abe could hear the pain in her voice as she answered again, "Yes, ma'am."

He heard a sharp inhalation, and his aunt said, "No, I don't think it's broken, but this is where it hurts?"

An answering whimper finally drove Abe away from the door and up the steep stairs to his room, where he hoped he would not be able to hear the girl's gasps of pain any more. He threw himself onto his bed and covered his head with his arms, blocking out the world for a while.

Soon enough, though, he heard his aunt calling his name. "Abimeal! Confound it boy, get back in here. I need your help."

When he returned to the kitchen, the first thing he saw was that his aunt was holding the girl's bare leg on her lap, the skin stretched taut and purpled with a massive bruise above her ankle. He turned away in embarrassment, trying to find somewhere else to direct his gaze. Betty's face eyes were closed tightly, and her face was grey, twin trickles of tears winding their ways down her cheeks.

Abe forced himself to meet his aunt's eyes. "Yes, ma'am?"

"Fetch me two pieces of stout kindling and then get a clean rag from beside the sink. We need to bind this up."

"Yes, ma'am." He hurried about, gathering the wood and cloth, and brought them back to his aunt.

"Tear the rag into strips," she directed, and he did as she told him. "I can't know whether this will help her injury at all, but I believe that it will make her more comfortable, at the least."

She positioned the kindling on either side of the girl's leg, then shook her head. "No, fetch another rag to wrap her leg first to protect her skin from the wood."

"Aye." As he brought the cloth back, he found Betty looking at him, a wan, grateful smile on her lips. Aunt Rosanna wrapped her leg and replaced the kindling.

"Now, wrap that first strip around her leg and tie it securely."

Abe reached past his aunt to do so, trying to ignore the wince on Betty's face as he tightened the binding.

"Same at the bottom," his aunt continued, and he did as she asked, eliciting another whimper from the girl. "Good," his aunt said approvingly. "That should do for the time being."

"Is it broken?"

"I can't find a break, but that may be just because there's so much swelling. As you can see, the girl's in a lot of pain, so I want to see if we can relieve that and bring balance to the humors—to drain some of the fluid from her leg."

Abe looked at her for a moment, aghast. "You don't mean to bleed her?"

His aunt scowled at him. "Nay, I am no surgeon, nor a barber. We'll bind her leg and lift it for the evening, and in the morning we'll see whether we need to call for their services."

"She's to spend the night here?"

"Of course," his aunt snapped.

"Oh, Miss Sawyer, that's not necessary," Betty said. "I am sure that Abe can help me to my lodgings—"

"Nonsense," Aunt Rosanna snapped. "You'll sleep in my bed, I'll take Abe's, and he'll sleep on the floor." She smiled at Abe. "It'll seem like old times, I'll wager, sleeping on a pallet again."

Chapter 12

The next morning, despite his weariness after carrying Betty, Abe was awakened by the wind rattling the panes of the window above him. For the first time since he'd come to live with his aunt, he could feel a chill in the air. He rose and peered out the window to find a landscape transformed by snow and ice. He went into the kitchen and added wood to the fire, sending up a satisfying shower of sparks.

He didn't often rise before his aunt, so it did not often fall to him to prepare breakfast, but he knew well enough what needed to be done. By the time he heard her making her way down the creaking stairs in the front room, the tea was steeping and he'd started melting a knob of bacon grease in the spider to fry eggs in.

"Nasty morning out there," Aunt Rosanna remarked as she sat down and Abe poured her tea.

"Yes, ma'am," Abe said mechanically. He realized with a start just how weary he still was when he noticed was still working on the basis of long habit. The eggs were already mostly cooked, and he'd prepared them the way that his father had liked, and not as his aunt preferred hers. With an inward sigh, he turned them over, pushing them to the side of the pan so that he could get hers started.

"Didn't get a chance yesterday with all the excitement to tell you where things stand with the woodcutters."

"Aye?" If he were being honest with himself, Abe had a hard time caring very much about the details of the deal after the events of the prior day, but he knew that they were important to his aunt.

"They're really not pleased with having to work around the trees bearing the King's mark instead of making a clean sweep of the lot, and demanded an extra two shillings out of each pound the timber fetches at the mill. I talked them down to a shilling of each pound, but 'Tis still a steep price, never mind the money lost to those trees still left standing."

Abe grimaced, aware of what his aunt was hinting at. "You think we should let them fell the mast trees, too, and take our chances with the surveyor."

She slurped at her tea. "I am not keen to take the chance of drawing attention to our precarious legal position. Fixing your mark to a contract giving them clear permission in writing to violate the law could have dire consequences."

She set the tea down and steepled her hands before her face for a moment. "Were it my grant, I would write the contract for just five shillings of each pound, not six, and verbally give them leave to cut it clear. The extra amount for the timber from those trees would more than compensate them for the lower rate."

She added, choosing her words carefully, "Of course, I am not suggesting that it would be prudent or wise for us to proceed thus with property that will eventually belong to you, and which at most I might manage until you are of age."

Abe thought for a moment, checking her eggs and flipping them onto a plate. He grabbed his own plate and got his eggs—a little bit dry and overcooked—and sat across the table from her.

"What's the penalty for taking the mast trees?" He frowned to himself and stood back up to pour his own tea.

"Typically, if the magistrate or the sheriff catches a woodcutter with mast trees, he will condemn them, meaning a total loss for the illegally taken trees. A couple of years ago, Governor Wentworth decided to make an example of a team over at Windsor, not people I know, but a man and his two sons, Deane by name."

She wrapped her hands around the cup of steaming tea for warmth. "The surveyor caught them red-handed, with hundreds of unsurveyed trees felled, of which some twenty-seven were of a size to have borne the King's mark. The governor rushed to the location, some one hundred and fifty miles from Portsmouth, and seized all that they'd felled, even that which would have been legal had it been surveyed."

She shook her head. "The governor secured a warrant for their arrest, and though the Deanes had flown by the time the warrant was in effect, they were soon enough caught and brought to Manhattan Island, in New-York, to await trial on the charges that the governor accused them of."

She chuckled. "Though the governor secured a conviction in the case, and they were fined in accordance with the statute, it developed that they had given everything they owned to a friend of theirs, a judge who was not involved in the case. As a result, they were bankrupt, and could pay nothing toward the fines levied against them. They were finally released from gaol last year, and they're probably back at it already."

She smiled at Abe. "The whole affair probably cost the governor more than it was worth to him, so he may have lost his appetite for prosecuting the mast laws, but there is always the danger that a particular incident will draw his attention."

Abe sighed. "I'll be honest, Aunt Rosanna. The risk doesn't sound like it's that high. The governor has only prosecuted one case in years, and that one ended badly for him?"

"Aye."

"Doesn't seem like enough reason to give up the additional money, or to pay the higher rate to the woodcutters."

His aunt raised an eyebrow at him and paused. "Very well then, it's settled. We can speak to the woodcutters as soon as this storm has passed." She began eating her eggs with newfound gusto.

From the other room, they heard Betty call, "Miss Sawyer? Can you help me for a moment, please?"

"Of course, child, just a moment." Swallowing a bite of egg, Aunt Rosanna stood and went to the door of her own room, where she paused for a moment before entering.

She emerged a few minutes later, the girl's arm draped over her shoulder, and helped her into a chair at the table. Abe hastily scraped the rest of his breakfast onto a fork and stood, finishing the last bite.

As he poured tea for the girl, he asked, "How do you take your eggs?"

"Oh, eggs? I usually eat them just boiled, but fried is fine. Turn them over, if you don't mind, and make sure that the yolks are cooked through."

"Certainly," Abe said, and busied himself at the hearth.

Betty looked through the window, sighing. "'Tis hard weather for my herd, though their winter coat is in, so they should stay warm enough, so long as they have the wit to stay dry under he shelter I've provided for them."

Aunt Rosanna asked, "They have food and water?"

"Aye, food they can uncover in the pastures—the snow is not so deep that they cannot root through it, though they like it better if they don't have to—and there is a creek that hardly ever freezes this early, and which runs right through their meadow."

Another gust rattled the window panes, and she added, "I only hope that the wind does not chill them. Were I uninjured, I'd be going out to check on them."

Aunt Rosanna snorted. "You're lucky that this boy found you when he did. Were you out in this still, we'd be putting another corpse into the graveyard, instead of welcoming another to the table."

The girl looked soberly at her. "I know, which is why I sent the raven for him."

"You 'sent' the bird to go and find Abimeal?"

"Aye. He was worried for me, and it both gave him something useful to do, and brought your nephew to where I was."

Aunt Rosanna had a serious frown on her face, and Abe was surprised to note that her expression bore some fear as well. In a low voice, she asked, "Miss Randall, I must ask you a very important question, and I will require an honest answer from you. Do you consort with the Devil, and do you derive your unnatural powers from some agreement with him? In short, are you a witch?"

Betty's mouth hung open for a moment, and Abe couldn't tell if it was out of surprise or actual amusement, but the girl burst into open laughter. Aunt Rosanna visibly swelled, as though preparing to explode, and Abe cringed on behalf of her target.

When the girl regained her power of speech, she said between renewed fits of giggles, "No, ma'am, nor are my 'powers' unnatural in the slightest. I merely speak with the animals that are my companions, and on occasion one of them gives evidence of understanding me; that is the extent of my communication with the raven."

Looking unsatisfied, Aunt Rosanna said stiffly, "In the old days, there were tests employed to ensure that a statement such as yours was the truth, but those days are past, so I must decide for myself whether I can believe you or not. While we may be obliged to suffer a witch to live, I cannot be expected to suffer one to live under my own roof."

After a shocked silence, Abe exclaimed, "Aunt Rosanna, you cannot possibly be serious in accusing Miss Randall of witchcraft as though we lived in Salem of a century ago. If you are going to send her out into the snow and the cold, I will leave as well."

Without having given the matter any thought, he heard himself add, "I can go and live in my father's old house just as happily as I live here in the village, and without all of your intrigues and schemes. The question of what to do with my father's estate can wait until the magistrate has had his say." His aunt's expression was stormy and her complexion nearly beet-red.

"Boy, you will not speak to your elders in such a tone. Why I've half a mind to fetch a switch and do for you what your mother never did! Had she striped your back when you were young enough to be taught—as I told her she needed to do—you would have proper respect for me, and gratitude for all I've done for you."

Betty spoke up, her voice quiet but firm. Aunt Rosanna glared at her as she spoke, but kept her silence. "I'll not be the cause of such violent family strife. Miss Sawyer, I assure you that I am no witch, nor possessed of any supernatural powers. I would gladly share with you all that I know about the ways of the wild animals with which I pass my days, and demonstrate that I do nothing at all out of ordinary experience to cause them to do the things that they do for me."

She turned to Abe. "My friend, you owe your aunt an apology. She knows not of what she speaks, 'Tis true, but she has provided you with a comfortable home and more family than most in our orphaned state may ever enjoy. She bound up my hurts, even when she harbored such suspicions against me, and that must count for something."

Abe's face burned with shame as he realized the truth of what she'd said. Aunt Rosanna had taken him in when she would have been wholly within her rights to have informed him of his father's death and sent him home to fend for himself. Where he was largely ignorant of the details of reaching agreements with woodcutters, she had taken on that responsibility without any evidence of personal gain.

The girl placed her hands on the table, saying, "I will take my leave now, as my poor goats must be tended to. They don't always have the sense to get under shelter, and though they have warm coats of fur, the damp and the wind can defeat that and leave them vulnerable to the cold." She started to stand up, gave a sharp cry of pain, and sat back down heavily.

Aunt Rosanna was out of her chair in a flash, kneeling beside the girl and taking her hurt leg into her hands. "Be still, child, and let me see whether you have hurt yourself further," she said with a hiss. "Nobody is going anywhere today, not in this weather. If my hens are bright enough to seek shelter from the storm, I feel certain that your goats can do likewise."

As her fingers worked along the length of the girl's shin, less swollen than it had been the previous day, she turned to Abe. "You'll be staying with me until you have reached the age where the law will permit you to manage your own affairs. After that, you are free to go, whether to your father's hovel or to build a home of your own. In the meantime, I have the responsibility to see to your care and safety."

Abe felt a flash of anger at her barb about his father's home, but he swallowed his reaction and let his aunt continue speaking.

She turned back to Betty. "In any event, your leg, whether it's broken or not, will not permit you to go and see to your goats any more than the weather out there will. You'll need to stay off of it for at least another day or two if it's not broken, and considerably longer if it is."

Her tone softened. "I apologize for what I said about you consorting with the Devil. It was uncalled for, regardless of my lack of understanding of your ways, and certainly we should never make such accusations without better evidence than not understanding something."

"Miss Sawyer, if you wish to put me to some sort of test to assure yourself that I am not a witch, I'll gladly subject myself to that test, if it will bring you peace in your concerns about me."

"Nay, it will not be necessary. The fact that you are willing to be subjected to a test means that you are either certain that you would pass such a test because you are wholly innocent, or that you are certain that you can outsmart any test that I might devise, because you are already so deep in the Devil's councils that my test would be futile."

She shared a smile with the girl. "I rather suspect the former, but if by some chance it is the latter, then I am already in mortal danger and no test will save me."

"Truly, we are at an impasse," the girl said, her answering grin merry. "I would offer you the assurance that I have no dealings at all with the Devil, but if I did, I would say the same, would I not?"

"Aye, so let there be no further accusations of witchcraft nor any playing at things that might be taken for the same," said Abe. "This house is too small for any sort of test in the old-fashioned sense, and far too small for a witch and an inquisitor to share."

He sniffed the air and turned back to the hearth with a gasp, and then chuckled. "In the meantime, 'Tis your eggs that have burnt, rather than any witch, and so I'll start again on your breakfast."

Chapter 13

The storm started to abate after a full day of wind and snow, and Abe slept poorly on the hard ticking under the window that rattled all night. They'd made light of the accusations in the end, but he couldn't help but think that there was something decidedly odd about the girl.

For one thing, there was the way that she had with the raven. They were, in his experience, inquisitive and even sometimes mischievous birds, but he had never heard of or encountered one before that appeared to listen to a person, much less one that could be bid to undertake a chore on the behalf of that person. Certainly, he'd heard ravens give a variety of calls, unlike the plain cawing and screeching of their smaller cousins, crows. But the range of sounds he'd heard Betty's companion utter was wider than Abe had ever heard before.

He tried to think back, to remember whether there were other instances of the girl being more than passing strange. She named her goats, but plenty of people named pets and even farm animals, so that was no particular indicator. Speaking as she had to the goat that they had chased through the house was eccentric, to be sure, but hardly evidence of witchcraft in any way.

In truth, it came back to the raven's preternaturally intelligent behavior in the girl's moment of need. Coming and finding Abe, and then leading him as though on a string to where the girl lay n desperate need of aid, was scarcely the act of a simple animal. ndeed, the more he thought about it, the more it disquieted him nd kept his mind racing.

A gust of wind gave the panes overhead a particularly 'icious shake, and he gave up going to sleep for the time being. ʒuided by the dim light of the dying fire, he rose and went into he kitchen, where he poked at the fire, amusing himself with the prays of sparks rising from the red-hot coals in the hearth.

He put another log on the fire and adjusted the coals so that hey embraced it, setting it ablaze, bringing the kitchen to life with ʒaping shadows and the pops and whistling sighs of the log as it ieated up and began to burn.

Sitting alone at the kitchen table in the quiet and dark iouse, he remembered the bag of money that he'd found before in he cupboard, and wondered whether it was still there. He arose nd opened the door to the cupboard, but in the shadowy half- ʒght of the fire in the hearth, he could not see into the back of the ompartment.

He reached in, sweeping his arm around until it encountered he leather satchel, which he drew out slowly, having half-believed hat it had been a product of his imagination. But here, in his hand, ʼ was again before his eyes. Its weight was solid in his hand, and he muted sound of metal on metal within proclaimed to the world hat it was full of money, more money than Abe had ever imagined ιying eyes upon.

He returned to the table with it and opened it. The dull leam of the coins within beckoned, and he tipped some of them ut onto the table. They clinked and rang against the wood and ach other, and Abe froze, hoping that the noise had not disturbed

Betty, just in the next room.

Hearing no movement from her, he returned to his consideration of the coins. There was a mix of everything from heavy gold guineas—not a lot of them, but more than he'd ever seen in one place before—to copper ha'pennies. There were quite a few crowns and half-crowns as well, reinforcing his notion that this was a considerable fortune.

He had the sudden recollection of the keen interest that his aunt had had in her brother's savings in that first day after his death, and realized that she hadn't asked about it since. He thought, with growing certainty, that she hadn't asked about it since because she had found it that day, and secreted it here.

He swept the coins up in his hand and returned them to the bag, unsure of how to approach this mystery with his aunt. With all of the suspicion and distrust already present in the house, it seemed better to let the question lie unasked for the moment.

It was certainly possible that she was merely acting as custodian for the estate, and hadn't said anything because that role was not formally hers yet. In that event, the money would come to him in due course, and he spent a few minutes daydreaming about what that could mean.

He knew that people who had money could do things like purchase land to work as a farm, or a horse to ride, or buy their way into an apprenticeship to a desirable career. Why, he supposed one could even buy a commission in His Majesty's Navy or Army, although the prospect of being called upon to enforce some future successor to the Stamp Act against his neighbors did not sound appealing.

Then there were the ordinary daily ways in which one could

spend money, if one had it. The sensation was so foreign to him that he had to give conscious thought to the question. Warmer boots, for one thing, or even a newer jacket—or both, if they weren't too dear. Meat for the table more often than once or twice a fortnight.

He could hire someone to tutor him in finer pursuits than woodcutting and chicken tending, perhaps even reading and figures. And then he could fill a shelf with books about subjects that would elevate his position in the world even further. He fairly trembled at the possibilities.

He had to remind himself, though, that he did not know for certain that the money was his father's savings, and even if it was, he didn't know how much latitude there was in the law regarding whether his aunt had to give it to him, or whether she might be able to keep it for herself.

He wasn't quite sure what she did to earn money-other than selling eggs-but her expenses couldn't be that high from what he'd seen in the time that he'd lived under her roof. Other than her extravagant use of firewood and meat more often than he was used to, she lived modestly, had apparently inherited the house, and bartered for what she didn't grow or collect for herself.

Was it possible that she had somehow earned that much money, and had been able to accumulate it through the same habits of frugality that her brother had practiced all his life? He thought back to the sale of the whole cask of eggs and rejected that thought. Unless she had some other source of income of which he was wholly unaware, the money had to have come from his father, one way or another.

He retied the drawstrings on the purse and slipped it back into the hiding place in which his aunt had secreted it. Whatever the source of the money, she had chosen for the moment to keep it a secret from him, so he must keep as a secret the fact that he knew of its existence.

When he finally managed to fall asleep, his dreams were full of increasingly bizarre ways that he was losing his father's fortune, culminating in Betty's raven flying away with it and taking it to Governor Wentworth, a shadowy, indistinct figure. The governor was flinging the coins to the ground, where each one sprang up into a new tree, at which point he rushed forward with an axe to cut the King's mark into each one.

The morning sun streaming brightly through the window woke him, and though the window was frosted over on the inside from the cold air that had settled over them in the wake of the storm, he could see out through the clear portions of the glass that there was a fairly impressive snowfall on the ground, its pristine surface was marked already with the tracks of small animals and birds.

He pulled on his warm clothes and ventured outside to check on his aunt's chickens. They were huddled together inside their shed, their feathers fluffed out to trap warm air next to their bodies, and he noted with amusement that they all looked as though they had no feet at all, so closely were they hunched down on their perches.

"Good morning, ladies," he said to them, and smiled gently at their soft answering calls. He noted that their water had frozen over in the night, and knew that he'd need to heat some water and bring it out to them. "We'll get that taken care of right away, ladies, and let's get you some nice cracked corn to get you warmed up as well."

As he was pulling the lid off the barrel of corn, he stopped suddenly, aware that he had just been indulging in the same practice for which Betty had been accused of witchcraft. He shook his head, chuckling to himself as he lifted the lid and cast corn out onto the floor, where the chickens hopped down and squabbled amongst themselves for their portions. The only difference, he thought, between Betty and himself was that she chose to speak with a bird of greater intelligence.

Aunt Rosanna had been at pains to explain that her chickens were smarter than some she had kept in the past. Among other evidence she cited was the fact that they would go to roost in the enclosed shed, instead of clinging to exposed tree limbs when it got cold, where they would freeze to death and drop like feathered stones in the night. Still, these birds were but chickens, and it would be charitable to call them anything like intelligent.

He looked in their straw-filled nest boxes and found a half-dozen eggs, icy cold to the touch. For as many hens as his aunt kept, he really thought that there ought to be more eggs, but it wasn't his business to be finding them wanting. She had assured him that come spring, there would be more eggs than they knew what to do with, and they'd be putting up eggs in fresh barrels, instead of having to raid their supplies in order to put enough on the table for themselves.

He gathered up what eggs there were and brought them inside, pausing at the door to stomp the snow from his boots, and then slipping them off to avoid tracking snow and ice through the house. He realized too late that it would be pretty well impossible for anyone to sleep through the noise that this process made, but he didn't figure that either his aunt or Betty would want to sleep much longer into such a bright and sunny morning.

He brought the eggs into the kitchen and set them in the bowl for later. Grabbing the kettle, he went out through the back door and filled the kettle with close-packed snow from the steps. Melt water dripped from one of the long icicles arrayed along the edge of the roof and splashed onto the back of his neck, eliciting a surprised yelp from him.

He heard a giggle from behind him in the kitchen and turned to see that Betty was up, standing with her injured leg safely tucked up, and leaning against the frame of the door to Aunt Rosanna's bedroom. "Good morning, Abe," she said, her eyes dancing with amusement.

"Good morning," he grumbled, and hung the kettle up on its crane. He ignored her while he stoked the fire and swung the crane over the flames. When that was done, he turned back to speak with her again. She had hopped one-legged to a chair, and was sitting at the table, looking quite pleased with herself.

Aunt Rosanna came into the kitchen then, looking bleary-eyed, with her hair wild from sleep. "That bed of yours, boy, I have no idea how I slept in it for so many years when I was younger." She sat down heavily and put her chin into her hand.

She noticed Betty sitting at the table then, and raised an eyebrow at her. "You, child, look far too pretty to have just been awakened by someone stomping on the floor."

laughed right out loud. "Miss Sawyer, I do own a mirror, and I know that my morning appearance is nothing like the way I go out into the world. Why, I should wonder whether your nephew hasn't had all of his illusions about girls spoiled in just the past two mornings."

Abe frowned. "I haven't any particular illusions about

girls to spoil," he said. In truth, he hadn't given the matter much thought, though he supposed that they did put more effort into their appearance and dressing before going into public than did men.

Betty gave him a shrewd look. "If you haven't any illusions, then I suppose I shall have to see about establishing some." Aunt Rosanna favored her with a tired frown, and Abe shook his head and pulled the crane with the kettle out of the hearth. The snow had melted, and the water was steaming well enough, so he used a folded-up rag to remove the kettle and stood up with it.

"I'm taking care of watering the chickens," he said and walked out, setting down the kettle to put his boots back on. As he laced them up, he could hear his aunt speaking to Betty.

"Once he's gone, we can speak plainly to one another, woman to woman," she said quietly.

"Oh? Please say your piece, Miss Sawyer. I do not think that he can hear us from the other room."

"Mind that you don't set your cap on that boy." Though he'd been raised better than to eavesdrop, Abe froze now, straining to hear. "He's got a lot more growing and learning to do before he can consider courting. Furthermore, it's my duty as his last living blood relation to ensure an adequate match for him. Unless I am very much mistaken about your fortunes, child, there are more suitable matches in this town for you."

"Miss Sawyer, I hesitate to say so while I am under your roof-even as a reluctant guest-but you forget yourself, ma'am. I will do as I wish, and I think you will find that Abe will do likewise."

"Miss Randall, as you say, you are a guest under my roof, and the obligations of hospitality bar me from giving that statement the response it deserves." Aunt Rosanna's tone was low and furious, and Abe shuddered in spite of himself. "We will have to agree to disagree for the duration of your confinement here, but you may rely on a continuation of this conversation after that time."

For the first time, Abe heard real anger in Betty's voice. "I look forward to that with the greatest anticipation, Miss Sawyer."

Moving as quietly as he could, Abe picked up the kettle and opened the door, working the latch carefully to minimize the noise it made as he closed it behind him. As chilly as the air was outside, it was more welcoming than the atmosphere inside the house.

Chapter 14

"There are some things that we must discuss, boy." Aunt Rosanna's voice was firm and businesslike. Abe was just back from assisting Betty in returning to her own abode, which had been both awkward and strangely pleasant. She'd insisted that she was able to make the trek, and though she'd had to lean heavily on him and keep her injured leg off the ground, they had together hobbled across the village to the house where she had a room.

His head was still buzzing slightly from the warm embrace that Betty had given him at her door, and the quick, warm sensation of her kiss on his cheek. He hadn't thought that he had any interest in involving himself with a girl, but he had to admit that it was terribly pleasant.

He pulled his head out of the clouds to answer. "Aye, Aunt Rosanna, I reckon that there are." He sat at the kitchen table where she awaited him.

"I've gotten Mister Howard to assist me in drawing up the contract that we will offer to the woodcutters. It incorporates the things that you and I already discussed with them and between ourselves. It does not address the question of the mast trees, but the rate we are offering them is based on the verbal agreement we have with them for including those trees."

Abe nodded. "Though I'm not eager to begin my career as

a grant holder by flouting the law, I confess that I do not see a more reasonable course available in this circumstance."

She frowned slightly when he called himself a grant holder, but said only, "You must put your mark here"—she pointed at the bottom of the page—"next to where I've put mine, as the presumed executor of your father's estate and as your presumed guardian."

He looked over the page of closely-spaced handwriting, wishing that he could read it for himself, instead of having to take his aunt's word for its contents. She dipped a quill in the inkwell and handed it to him. He signed with an "X," and she took the quill from him and signed her own name next to his mark, adding some words in smaller handwriting below it.

Seeing his glance at the writing, she said, "That is only explaining that I have witnessed you making your mark, and that I vouch for your intent and identity." He nodded, satisfied, and she sprinkled the signatures with her sander, waiting a moment for the ink to dry, and then set the page aside.

Motioning to it, she said, "I did include a clause that obliges us to have a representative of your interests check on their progress from time to time, to ensure that they are cutting the trees agreed to, and no others. I anticipate that you may spend a day or two out there every fortnight, and when necessary, you may need to stay in your father's old house."

Abe nodded. Though the old house would likely be crowded with memories of somewhat happier times, it would also be a comfort to spend some time alone in more familiar surroundings.

"Now," she said, and her tone had instantly taken on a frosty edge. "About that girl. In addition to my concerns about her powers over her raven, which she has not explained to my satisfaction, I can tell that she has designs on you, and that concerns me. I would ordinarily not insert myself into the private affairs of two young people, but in this case, I have a responsibility to you that I inherited when I offered to take you in at the time of my brother's death."

She sighed. "In due time, you will become a relatively wealthy man, and much as it pains me to say so, wealthy men attract a certain sort of girl, one who sees a way to her own comfort and prosperity through playing on the affections of men with money."

Abe opened his mouth to object—Betty was the furthest thing he could imagine from the sort of grasping, opportunistic person she was describing—but Aunt Rosanna held up her hand, forestalling his comments. "Let me finish, please."

He closed his mouth, but frowned at her sullenly, scarcely listening to what she had to say next. "This sort of girl can be flattering to a man's ego, fawning over his words and ingratiating herself to him in all manner of ways, small and large." She smiled grimly. "You must learn how to avoid such girls and to recognize when one has set her snare for you."

He could not be restrained any further. "Betty—Miss Randall—isn't that way at all. She's more concerned with the welfare of her goats than she is about her own comfort, and I suspect that she prefers the company of that raven to that of any man at all."

His aunt smiled indulgently. "So it may seem to you now. But I witnessed her looking at you with a certain mercenary gleam in her eye. Furthermore, as a man of means, you should be matched up with a partner who can add to your holdings, not diminish them. There is no lack of suitable girls in this colony, and I am certain that when the time is right, we can find one who would make your father proud of you."

Abe sat with his mouth hanging open, amazed at the gall of this woman. He finally recovered sufficiently to ask, his tone sharp and impatient, "What 'we' is there in my finding and wooing a bride?"

His aunt chuckled. "Why, I think you'll find that I can be of great assistance in helping you to make the right introductions and set the correct criteria for your marriage arrangements. I may not be a grant holder in my own right, but I have had dealings with some of the leading figures in this area, and I may flatter myself to say that I can name at least a half-dozen girls who are of a marriageable age, or who will be soon enough."

Abe snapped, "You presume that I have any interest at all in marrying, never mind marrying one of your proper girls from the right family. In fact, it may sound like a sort of blasphemy to your ears, but I am not even particularly interested in your claim that I will be a man of wealth. A roof over my head, food on my plate, and work enough to keep my days full, and I have all that I need."

She smiled at him, shaking her head with open amusement. "Oh, you innocent babe," she said. "Soon enough you will discover the charms of both wealth and of the fairer sex. In the meantime, I will faithfully fulfill my duties to my brother, whether or not you want my help."

He scowled at her, and she shook her head. "I knew that you were a spoiled child, but I had never noticed how headstrong you'd become in the bargain."

She made a dismissive gesture with her hands. "Regardless of your present shortcomings, though, you have the means to improve yourself, and I intend to ensure that you are availed of them. I have

hought better of my initial intent to teach you myself, and I will
be arranging a tutor for you, to teach you to read and give you
he rudiments of business mathematics. You ought to be able to do
ums and assess a contract on your own, whether or not I am here
o hold your hand and do it all for you."

His scowl softened just a bit. She had somehow found the
ne thing that he actually did want, and he was at least marginally
rateful to her for that. "You ought to learn some of the niceties of
ocial life as well, but this village is not a place for that, nor do I even
now enough of those aspects of a proper education to attempt to
each you myself."

She gave a small, triumphant smile. "I expect that between
our responsibilities around the house, your duties out on the grant,
nd your lessons, you will be so busy that our Miss Randall will
ind you quite dull and difficult to find time with. Besides, she can
ardly chase you with her leg as it is, and by the time that has
ealed up, I anticipate that you'll be far too busy to care."

Chapter 15

"'T is nothing short of shameful that you cannot read already, you know," Aunt Rosanna said. "I suspected that your father was neglecting your education in favor of his own pursuits, but it was not really my place to say so."

She sighed. "Now that it has become my place to do something about it, I am dismayed to find that you are starting from a place of utter darkness." Frowning, she added, "At least I was able to secure a decent tutor for you. He will be here shortly, so get yourself dressed and cleaned up. There's no need for your appearance to cause as much talk as your ignorance."

Abe scowled, but said nothing. His mind was elsewhere, as Betty had hobbled up behind him with an improvised crutch and accosted him while he was on his way to fetch water the prior day. "I take it that your aunt spoke to you about me?"

He wasn't quite sure what to say, so he settled on the simplest approach—the truth. "Aye. She has some wild theories about you and has undertaken to keep me occupied and far from you." He shrugged. "I think that she means well, perhaps, but she doesn't always have the kindest manner about her."

Betty snorted. "You've said a mouthful there, for sure. Well you may assure her that I will be back in my fields with my goats and will be out of sight, and I may presume, out of mind, soon enough. My leg is healing up, and with the use of this"-she waved the crutch in his general direction-"I've been out to see the poor wretches. They are as eager for my company as I am for theirs."

"I'm glad to hear that you are healing well, and that your companions weathered the storm." He wasn't sure what else to add to that, and awkwardly stepped around her to get to the well.

"I'll send the raven if I need you again," she called after him, a mysterious smile on her lips. "That will be sure to further endear me to your aunt."

Abe smiled over his shoulder at the girl. "Aye, that it will."

He'd seen the bird around town even more often than he'd seen her, since she'd returned to her own home, and it had always seemed to take a particular interest in what he was doing. He had no patience for his aunt's claim that the girl was a witch, but there was something decidedly unsettling about the way that the raven looked at people.

Now, though, he was combing back his hair, and donning the clean breeches that Aunt Rosanna had procured for him. She had not yet insisted that he don a waistcoat, but she did force him to wear proper stockings and shoes, though the buckles were plain ironwork, and not the silver she'd wanted for him. After grumbling about the rates that silversmiths demanded, she'd grimly settled for the less expensive option, her mouth pursed almost comically.

The shoes made his feet hurt, being new, and the breeches were itchy. Their wool was warm when he was in the chilly outdoor air, but she forbade him to wear them other than to church and back, until now. Inside her overheated house, the warmth of the breeches was nearly enough to make him swoon.

He sighed and looked at himself in the glass that she had

supplied. He looked as much the part of a gentleman as he supposed he could manage, and when the anticipated rap came at the door, he stuck his tongue out at his reflection and rose to go answer it.

The man at the door was the son of the pastor, a fellow named Gershom, and while he and Abe had had little to do with one another prior to this, Abe was respectful of the other man's learning. "Come in, please, Gershom. My aunt would like a word with you, I'm sure, and then we can begin at our table."

"Certainly, Abimeal. I am glad to be of service in your education." Gershom bowed slightly and entered. He removed his hat and knocked the ice from his boots with his cane, an affectation that Abe had always thought a bit overdone. However, when the man turned to enter the kitchen, Abe saw him lean on the cane for a bit of extra support, and he wondered at the cause of the man's infirmity.

"Ah, Mister Cooper, how kind of you to come and aid my nephew. I trust that your father is well?"

"Yes, Miss Sawyer. As I told your nephew, it is my pleasure to spread the light of knowledge, passing along what was granted to me."

"Aye." She nodded approvingly. "As I told you before, I would undertake to teach him myself, but I fear that my gifts lie in other areas than in the patient field of teaching."

"Of course," Gershom said. "May we begin, Miss Sawyer?"

Aunt Rosanna nodded and took the cue to leave them in peace. She pulled on her cloak, saying, "I'll be off, then, to the mercantile for some necessaries."

After she'd left, Gershom sat across from Abe and said, "I've brought the book your aunt asked me to provide to you—it's just up from Boston, the New-England Primer. We won't spend a lot of time with it today, but when you're ready, you'll have it."

Abe accepted the book, marveling at the unblemished cover and the crisp printing. "I've brought some paper and a quill as well as your own ink and sander, though you won't need those for a while yet, either."

He smiled. "'Tis mostly useful for documents where you must make your mark, and not for practicing your penmanship."

Abe's smile faltered a bit. "I am to learn a proper hand, as well?"

Gershom nodded. "Everything in its time, don't worry. For today, let us discuss just the forms of the letters."

Abe attended the lesson as closely as he could, though his mind wandered when Gershom went on a tangent about letters not used for English, but only in the Greek, which he apparently loved beyond all reason. Abe could imagine no possible use for Greek in his pursuits, and was thinking again about the embrace he'd shared with Betty when he suddenly looked up, after Gershom said, " . . . and I learned my Greek at university in London last year—"

Abe interrupted, "You've been to London?"

Gershom frowned slightly. "Aye, as I expect someday you may do as well, should you wish to pursue your studies or advance in business."

Abe leaned forward eagerly. "What was it like, to sail across the ocean?"

Gershom smiled wryly and said, "Mostly, it was pretty dull. When it was not dull, though, it was terrifying, as a great storm came up and nearly brought us to founder. Thankfully, the trip back home was less exciting, and I had books to keep me company, when I could keep my food down."

He shuddered in memory. "For the most part, travelling to London is something that every gentleman of these Colonies should probably do once in their lives, but those who make a career of travel on the seas are a breed apart."

"What was London like?" Abe had never been particularly entranced by the thought of travel before, but sitting here, in the presence of someone who had actually gone to these faraway places fired his imagination.

Gershom thought for a moment before answering. "Well, as you would likely imagine, it is very large, and the number of people one encounters is truly staggering. Most are decent and good, like the people you know here, but a few whom I encountered thought ill of me, only because I came from New-England."

He scowled slightly at the memory. "They could tell me apart from their own countrymen by my manner of dress, and to some degree by my speech, which sounds somewhat different from the way they speak."

He shook his head, his lips pursed in disapproval at the memory. "They are very much aware of a man's origins in London, and if they perceive you to be from a distant part of the Crown's dominion, many of them will have nothing at all to do with you."

Abe frowned in response. "Are we not all equally subjects of the Crown?"

"There are as many subjects of the Crown on this side of the Atlantic as in Britain, I have heard it said, but they heed us not when we say that we deserve representation in the Parliament, and some go so far as to say that these colonies will remain forever dependent upon the mother country for many of our necessary trade goods, never mind defense against the depredations of the Indian nations and the enemies of the Crown in Europe."

Abe's eyebrows rose up on his forehead. "Are there really that many in the American colonies?"

"Aye, though I suppose that it depends upon whether we count the slaves among our numbers as owing fealty to the King."

"I had been given to understand that their sole fealty was to their masters." Abe's father had never had good things to say about the institution of slavery, even though Abe had always privately thought that it would be nice to have someone about who would not refuse chores, and who was obliged to follow instructions without rebellion.

"'Tis true that they are required to obey the commands of those who have imported or bought them, but they are also subject to the commands of the Crown, in addition, just as we may be in the employ of another man, but may be required to set aside that employment if the needs of the Crown or its representatives should require it."

"I suppose that I understand that," Abe said, though his tone was still doubtful.

They heard the front door swing open then, and Aunt Rosanna came into the house, laden with parcels. "I've the makings of a proper supper here, should you be interested in staying, Mister Cooper."

She set down her parcels and the rucksacks she'd brought back. "However, there is some family business that Abe and I must attend to first, if you will excuse us."

"Certainly, Miss Sawyer. As you wish. I would be most grateful to join you for supper afterward." He bowed and excused himself.

When the man had stepped into the front room, Aunt Rosanna sat down wearily in one of the kitchen chairs. "Well, 'Tis official. The magistrate has appointed me as the executor for your father's estate and has given me the responsibility to raise you as though you were my own."

Chapter 16

Now that the question of their relationship was formally settled, it seemed to Abe that his aunt was just the slightest bit less on edge. He'd had one night out at his old house, spending most of the evening cleaning and re-seasoning the rusted spider there. The woodcutters judged the swamp to still be insufficiently frozen, but if the cold continued unbroken for another week, they could start work in that woodlot.

Meanwhile, they had made substantial progress towards clearing the strip agreed upon, including most of the trees that had been marked by the deputy surveyor. The marks had all been mysteriously chopped away in the process of felling them, and they rested on sledges alongside all the others from the section. Only their size betrayed them now, and the closer they came to being finished products, the harder it would be for anyone to detect the violation of the law.

Abe said nothing about it to the men, noting only that they had worked where they were supposed to, and had not exceeded the terms of the written contract otherwise.

He approached the chief of the woodcutters. "When will these be moved to the mill?"

"Oh, I reckon as soon as the snow is deep enough again." Much of the first storm's accumulation had been blown away by frigid winds. Abe nodded. "Once the sledges can pass onto the road and thence to the mill, these sticks are their problem, and not ours."

Shouts and several loud cracks drew their attention then, as one of the tall, straight trees that had borne the King's mark began to topple. The woodcutters had chopped it partway through on one side and were driving a wedge into it on the opposite side, until the fibers of wood were parted in a series of loud ruptures.

With each pop, the tree leaned further and further into the cut, until it gave one last almighty crack and the base parted entirely. The trunk was started on its ponderous way to the ground, and as it gathered speed, Abe could hear the whistling of the air through its boughs.

When it finally hit the ground, the earth under Abe's feet jumped, followed by a blast of wind from the passing of the crown through the air to the former forest floor. Abe felt a moment of shock at the realization of what the massive impact would do—had done—to a man who was unfortunate enough to be caught in its path.

A part of him was grateful to know that his father's death had been an instantaneous extinguishment, and another part of him was shaken to the core at how quickly a man's life could be snuffed out. He felt humbled and diminished in the face of such awesome forces.

He took a deep breath and shook off the feeling as well as he could. Curious, he approached the new-fallen tree, now surrounded by men removing the branches with axes. As some of the lower limbs were as big around as an ordinary tree, this was not a minor undertaking, and the massive trunk lay suspended on the splintered stumps of some of them, as far off the ground as the height of a man.

He noticed then that the trunk had snapped about halfway up its length, and he frowned unhappily. Pointing at the rupture, he said, "This one appears to have been substantially reduced in its size by breakage." He glanced around at some of the other large trunks, noting, "It looks like the same and worse has happened to many of these. Will they still fetch as high a price at the mill?"

The man shrugged. "They will fetch more than they would have, had they remained standing."

"Fair enough, but is there no way to prevent them from coming to grief as you fell them?" Abe was not pleased with the man's offhand manner. The money did not bother him so much as the waste. A single beam of stout lumber, he'd often heard his father say, could support the whole of a long roof, while shorter, less intact pieces could only be used for flooring planks or wall studs.

The woodcutter looked thoughtful for a moment and said, "Might could have done, but they're cut now. We can't put them back up now."

Abe scowled. "I will ensure that we are more exact in the instructions that we include in any future contract, then, and that we include appropriate incentives for you and your crew."

The man nodded briskly, clearly nonplussed to be spoken to so directly by Abe. "As you like it." He turned away dismissively, and Abe decided in that moment that there would be no future contract with this man, if he could not be bothered to care about the quality of his work.

He turned away from the scene of the confrontation himself, walked back to the road, and started for his aunt's house. The old house was secure, and everything in its place for his next visit, and he was now suddenly eager to speak with his aunt to see if anything could be done to improve the work of the woodcutters.

As he walked, he found his thoughts returning time and time again to the moment when the huge tree had fallen to earth. Had his father been struck down by the main trunk of the tree that had felled him, or had a broken branch transfixed him to the ground like a grotesque doll on a peg? Had his father suffered, or had he actually been killed so quickly that he hadn't even seen his doom approaching? What had his final moments been, and his last thoughts?

Abe shook himself, forcing his mind to stop dwelling on these horrible thoughts. In desperation, he began reciting some of the lessons that Gershom had set for him in the past week. The primer had clearly been designed for use by small children in a school, rather than a man nearly of age with an individual tutor, but the rhymes were, at least, easy enough to remember.

They all sounded more like something he would hear on Sunday in church than anything he was inclined to say himself, but he let them trickle through his mind, a welcome distraction from his earlier morbid thoughts.

"In Adam's fall/We sinned all . . . , Heaven to find/The Bible mind . . . , Christ crucified/For sinners died . . . , The Deluge drowned/The Earth around . . . " On and on the rhymes went, each supposed to summon to his mind the characteristic of a specific letter. In truth, he was doing reasonably well at memorizing the letters, but the rhymes had little to do with it.

He had reached "Young Samuel dear/The Lord did fear" when a raven soared over him from behind, banking and circling around to look at him. He briefly inclined his head courteously to

he bird, saying, "Good day to you, and a pleasant day to your
nistress, when you see her."

The animal pumped its wings powerfully and flew on its
vay. Abe shook his head ruefully. "The girl has me talking to
nimals much as she does, and with as much effect," he said aloud.
And now she has me talking to myself as well."

The wind had been no more than a breeze all day, but it
tarted to pick up as he walked, and now a mischievous breeze
lipped under his cloak and gave him a sudden chill. He shivered
nd pulled the cloak tighter around his body.

In addition to the sturdy working clothes his aunt had
rocured for him, he wore a pair of old boots of his father's that
e'd found, with toes stuffed with rags as much for warmth as for
t. Indeed, his feet were about the only part of him that was not
hilled by the passing wind.

A break in the clouds let a ray of afternoon sunlight fall on
im, but it did little to warm him, so he walked faster, hurrying to
eturn to the welcome heat of Aunt Rosanna's home, benefiting
om the effort of moving faster.

As he reached the village and approached his aunt's house, he
aw that the raven was, again, sitting on a tree outside the upstairs
vindow, turning its head curiously this way and that. He walked
round the house to stand under the tree.

"Are you looking for me, perchance?" The bird looked down
t him, fixing him with one bright black eye. It looked him over
or a long moment before it returned its attention to the window.
be shook his head and returned to the front of the house, reciting
ne last of the letter couplets to himself as he opened the door.
'Zacchaeus he/Did climb the tree/Our Lord to see."

He shook his head at the ridiculous lengths to which the book's authors had gone for a simple rhyme, and bent to remove his boots after knocking the snow and ice from them.

Aunt Rosanna called from the kitchen, "How is their progress?"

"Good morrow to you, too," Abe said under his breath, but aloud he answered, "'Tis quite satisfactory, though they are spoiling what seems to me to be a lot of the trees they cut by letting them fall so far that they break and splinter. It would be good to have some written clarification for them to rely upon for our expectations of the condition of the lumber when it arrives at the mills."

"Oh, there already is, Abe. It's all spelled out how much they might earn by delivering all trunks substantially intact, along with a schedule of decreases, should they fail to do so."

"That is excellent news, and I only wish that I could have read the contract for myself, so that I would not have to go back out to the chief of the woodcutters and explain to him that I could not read what he was required to do." He frowned. "Is there any chance that we could invite Gershom over more often, that I may learn to read more quickly?"

Chapter 17

A be sat at the kitchen table, sipping his tea and watching through the window as the snow fell, the morning half-light lending a blue cast to everything outside. He nodded to himself, satisfied. The timber would be off to the mill soon, and no longer sitting on his father's grant.

Aunt Rosanna slumbered yet in her room, the dimness of the cloud-filtered light not yet having penetrated her consciousness. Abe awoke at about the same time every morning, shortly after sunrise, regardless of how much light intruded into his bedroom. As the winter darkness deepened, he'd even been waking up before sunrise.

His regular, comfortable routine now included the morning chores of stoking and feeding the fire in the kitchen hearth, gathering and melting snow, if there was no water left from the prior day, and making tea. These chores had even become a sort of throat-clearing ritual for whatever would follow each day. Once his aunt arose, he'd get their morning eggs going in the spider, and after breakfast, he'd clean up and then go tend to the chickens.

They were hardly laying at all now, and Aunt Rosanna had told him that they wouldn't really start again until springtime. When the nests didn't yield enough eggs for their daily needs, he'd take a lantern down to the cellar and fetch out preserved eggs to supplement the fresh ones. He was pleasantly surprised to discover that he could taste no difference between the fresh and preserved eggs, and he marveled at the ability to keep them safe by such a simple expedient.

On a snowy day like today he had his reading and writing practice to look forward to, and he had reached the point where he was genuinely eager to pick up his quill, or even the dour little primer. He now had all his letters learned, and could even sound out a few simple words, but there were some letter combinations that just made no sense, until Gershom explained them.

He knew better than to bother Aunt Rosanna with a question about how to make sense of an "h" following a "t" in a word?—would one pronounce them in order, "tu-huh," or did they combine to make some other, unpredictable sound? His aunt had none of Gershom's patience in explaining why words were made the way they were.

The one time he had asked—what on earth was he to make of the combination of "g," "h," and "t?"—she'd looked at the page, snapped, "That's 'right,' boy," which had led to several minutes of confused questions and increasingly irritated answers. It would have been funny, he realized, if she hadn't gotten so frustrated that the veins in her neck stood out and her face turned as red as a rooster's wattle. After that mutually disagreeable discussion, he resolved to wait for Gershom's next visit to puzzle out any particular word that stumped him.

In the meantime, he enjoyed flipping through the primer, picking out words that he did know, and examining the woodcut drawings. He could see that the printing process did not yield terribly detailed pictures, but they were still objects of fascination.

A profile image of the King himself, recognizable from its

similarity to the impressions on many of the coins he'd seen in the sack of money, had his attention this morning, and he was still looking at it minutely when his aunt came out of her room, stretching and yawning.

"A good morning to you, Aunt Rosanna," he said. "Looks like a good day to stay inside and tend to our indoor chores, eh?"

She favored him with a faint frown and wordlessly bent to make her own tea. Abe turned back to his book, opening it to a random page. It happened to be the alphabet page, whose words he already knew by rote memory, even if he couldn't sound them all out on the printed page yet.

"A cat doth play/And after slay." The "f" and "s" in the second line looked the same in the printing, which had confused him a great deal until Gershom had explained the idea of the "long s." It made no sense at all to Abe, but Gershom had practically waxed poetic as he described its noble descent from the perfection of the Greek alphabet. All Abe knew was that it made for just one more thing that he had to memorize as he was learning how different words looked on the page.

It wasn't the only thing that had caused Abe frustration in his lessons. Fine handwriting was, as far as he was concerned, a matter of witchcraft with the quill. He was well-enough satisfied to get the pen to make shapes that were recognizable as the specific letters he intended, but Gershom insisted that he practice making nonsense loops and various kinds of curved lines, "to train your hand in the motions needed to produce the letters."

His tutor had examined a sheet of such meaningless marks, sighing. "If you had a metal nibbed pen, we could make your hand even finer, but if you practice enough with the quill, you can come close to the ideal roundhand in time." Gershom seemed to think that it was only a matter of repeating the same lesson enough times, and Abe would just naturally learn how to write as nicely as he did himself.

His outdoor chores completed, Abe sat across the table from where his aunt was knitting a new stocking for him and bent to his practice. He knew in his heart that the most he could hope for was legibility, and even that was elusive. However, he knew that it was important to be able to write an easily-read page of instructions or even legal agreements, so he kept at it, his tongue at the corner of his mouth as he concentrated.

Referring back to the example of "Italick Letters" at the beginning of the primer, Abe decided to hand copy the alphabet rhymes for practice. He wasn't sure that Gershom would approve of him using the type letters as his exemplars, but he wanted very much to get past the rote practice of meaningless patterns in ink on the page, and on to actual writing.

He was halfway through "Thy Life to Mend/This Book Attend" when a crisp knock at the door surprised him. His aunt jerked her head toward the front room and said, "You answer the door. I am not yet dressed, and no visitor needs to see me in this state." He bit back the reply that sprang to mind-that he was hardly more dressed than she-and pushed his chair back from the table with a loud scrape across the wood floor.

As he stood to go answer the door, he bumped the inkwell, knocking it over onto the page he had been writing on. Thankfully, the ink had spread across the page, but not yet over its edges. Scowling at his clumsiness, he carefully picked up the ruined page, curving it so as to confine the pool of ink to its center, and tossed it nto the fire.

It leapt up in a cheerful burst of orange flame atop the hot coals, and Abe turned away to go to the door. He opened it to find the woodcutters' chief standing there, looking pleased with himself. "A good morning to you, Mister Sawyer. I just thought you would like to know that the timber we've cut is now on its way down the highway to the mill. It's now no trouble of ours if the King's men detect that the logs were not legally taken."

His pique at the man's careless attitude in felling the most valuable timber forgotten in the pleasure he felt at the news, Abe nodded. "This is good news indeed, and it calls for a celebration. Can I offer you a drink?"

The man's face lit up, and Abe stepped aside to welcome him into the house. "Do you take milk with your tea?"

The woodcutter looked confused for a moment, and then downcast. "I, er, I'll take milk, I suppose." He grimaced. "I had thought that you meant, you know, a drink."

Abe smirked and nodded. "Ah, yes, sorry for the confusion. That won't happen here, I assure you." He grinned openly. "My aunt keeps no spirits around, nay, not even cider or ale."

The woodcutter grimaced and said, "Do you know, I just remembered that my team is waiting for me, and so I should not pause in our journey to deliver the lumber. In addition, 'Tis blocking most of the thoroughfare, and though there is little other traffic on the roads today, that seems like a generally unfriendly act."

He paused, his hand resting on the door handle, and turned back to say, "I do wish I could accept your hospitality—perhaps another time?" Abe smiled at him. "Perhaps. I look forward to it. A safe journey to you then, and I hope that our timber fetches top prices at the mill. From what little I know of these things, it is of good quality, and enough quantity to manage the raising of a large house or a small barn."

The man smiled back. "You are a quick study, Mister Sawyer. We will make a woodcutter out of you yet."

Abe smiled grimly. "I think not, after my father's doom, but I am applying myself to learning the business as well as I can anyway."

"A wise lad. I will be back shortly with a report and the proceeds of the sale."

"Aye, see you soon." As he closed the door, Abe wondered at his aunt's wisdom at letting the woodcutter handle the financial end of the deal, but when they'd discussed it, she had pointed out that it provided a degree of separation between themselves and the sale of the illicit timber. He wasn't convinced that the danger was particularly acute, but had to trust his aunt's instincts about the trustworthiness of the woodcutter.

Chapter 18

It was another crisp winter morning, the sun glinting off the snow which lay thickly on the branches of the trees around Aunt Rosanna's house. The well-worn paths between the house and the chickens' shelter and around to the cellar door were icy in the morning chill, but Abe knew to be careful as he moved around.

He'd attended to their morning hot water, collected the five eggs they'd laid, and spread a treat of cracked corn across the hard-packed snow outside their shelter. They came racing out, intent on finding every trace of their favorite treat. He knew, though, that once their excitement had died down and they'd returned to the comfort of their shelter, the squirrels would emerge from the branches overhead and scour the ground for any particle of missed corn.

He brought the eggs inside and set them on the table to cook for breakfast, and then gathered up the buckets to fetch the day's water. Outside the front door, Betty's raven awaited, cocking his head at Abe curiously as he came out of the house. "Good morrow to you, dear raven," Abe said, his tone belying the formality of his words. "What word from yonder chief of your domain?"

The raven bobbed its head and emitted a sound very like a chuckle, before spreading its wings and flying away, seemingly satisfied. Abe shook his head and took to the road, empty buckets swinging from his hand. The village was quiet and peaceful under its coat of white, though the road was a riot of churned up frozen forms from the passage of horses, carriages, and other pedestrians. He noted a number of crows harassing a larger bird—some sort of hawk, it looked to Abe's unpracticed eye—and a chipmunk making its way hesitantly from one side of the road to the other.

In the distance, at the well, he saw a figure working to draw water up. As he came nearer, he saw that it was old Ephram, muttering under his breath as he raised and dropped the bucket to crack the ice at the bottom of the well.

Abe grinned at the old man as he arrived. "Should you like me to take a turn at it, sir?"

"Aye, boy, and well you should, so often does that aunt of yours leave this work for others to do before she comes out for her water."

Abe smiled without acknowledging the instructions his aunt had given to that very effect, and took the rope from Ephram's hand. He pulled it, hand over hand, a few feet from the bottom of the well, and then let it drop, careful to balance the need to crack the ice against the risk to the bucket itself. After the third repetition of this process, he was rewarded with the sound of a splash, as the water surged up past the broken ice far below.

He handed the rope to Ephram with a flourish, and the old man took it, his muttering no less dark. Abe heard just a snatch of it—"he thinks he's quite the macaroni, doesn't he?"—and turned away so that the man wouldn't see him snickering behind his hand. Nothing, it seemed, would satisfy the grumpy old man.

After Ephram had filled his own water buckets from the well and taken his leave-without so much as a "thankee"-Abe was in the process of filling his buckets when he heard a horse coming down the frozen road at a pretty good rate of speed. Looking up, he was surprised to see the chief of the woodcutting crew mounted, as he did not expect that the man could afford a horse.

The woodcutter spotted Abe at the well and drew up short beside him. He seemed out of breath as he said, "I am glad to find you away from your aunt's house. I came as quickly as I could to warn you that the surveyor came around yesterday to the mill where we sold your timber, and condemned the logs as belonging to the King's Woods."

A chill ran over Abe at the man's words. "What does that mean, exactly?"

"The surveyor has placed the King's mark on the lumber, and none may take it for private use, save for a fine be paid, or the violator sent to gaol for a year."

He must have seen Abe's face go white, as he added quickly, "The violators who stand accused and may be charged, should the magistrate choose to act, are the mill owners who have possession of the timber, not those who cut it, nor those from whose land it was taken. Of course, the mill owners may choose to inform the magistrate of the source of the timber, in which case, we may yet have some share of the trouble."

"Your words do not provide me with any assurance," Abe said. "I thought that the surveyor and the governor had been satisfied to assess fines, and then release the timber they deemed to have been taken in violation of the law, without any further action."

"Aye, that has been their habit, until now. I would venture to guess that the governor has noticed that there is money to be made in assessing these fines more often, and from as many parties as he can ensnare. There never was a royal office holder who could resist the opportunity to use his office for personal gain. They come here and eat out our substance, leaving us with nothing to feed our families or better our position."

"Is there no remedy, no appeal?"

The man snorted. "On what basis? The mill owners have plainly violated the law of the King's Woods and the mast tree regulations. Should they convey to the governor and his magistrate from whence they acquired this timber, there is little question but that I and my team have likewise participated in a clear violation."

He frowned at Abe. "It is just possible that no magistrate in the land would bring an action against a boy not yet of age-advised only by his aged and unstable aunt-but I only thought it fair to give you the word that you may need to be prepared to join me in the wind until the governor's attention wanders to some other lucrative extraction."

"So you will fly?"

"Indeed, until the matter is settled. Don't worry after the progress on your timber. We have completed most of the work in the swamp already, and I anticipate little difficulty in removing what we have already felled there before the danger is too keen. I am but keeping my baggage packed and my feet light, in case an actual need arises."

Abe nodded. "I do appreciate you bringing these unwelcome tidings to me. I will share them with my aunt, to ask her guidance as to what we should do to prepare for any necessary action."

He began lowering the bucket back down into the well, and then stopped. "We need not fear that you will send word to he magistrate of the source of the timber in question, in order to shield yourself from prosecution, or else earn leniency?"

The woodcutter shot Abe a wounded look. "Nay, I would never do such a thing, particularly not with the immediate prospect of further profitable work in your service." Abe remembered his determination to give the man no further work, and realized that he would likely have no option but to reward his loyalty, should it prove reliable.

Abe sighed and continued lowering the bucket. "I appreciate your discretion, sir, and I will await further news of you regarding the action taken by the magistrate."

"Aye, I will keep you informed. Just to be clear, however, the magistrate has not yet committed to take any action at all, and 'Tis even possible that the surveyor will opt not to refer all the violations he discovers for prosecution. The word from other mills that he has raided is that he has been most selective, and the swift payment of a 'fine' is a sure way to avoid referral to the magistrate."

Abe scowled. "Is all corruption so open and unambiguous?"

"Nay, some of it is far more stealthy, and some is even more unhidden. If a man is deep in the councils of the governor, he may do as he pleases. Why, there is a rumor that one of the deputy surveyors that Governor Wentworth has appointed to draw a salary from the King has actually left these shores to return to England. It seems unlikely that he can discharge his duties from that remove, but he will doubtless continue to collect the King's half-crowns for as long as the King's crown is secure."

Abe acknowledged the wordplay with a half smile and began raising the bucket back out of the well, then frowned, asking,

"What check is there on such abuse?"

"Only the vigilance of the King and his officers, which appears to be a weak bulwark against the opportunities that stir the souls of the dishonest."

Abe nodded, still frowning. "It may be that we here in the Colonies will need to take some action to provide for better guardians than that against this sort of misconduct."

"Aye, but so long as the King himself tolerates it, there seems little we can do." The woodcutter wheeled on his horse and waved his farewell, spurring the animal to return in the direction from which he'd come.

Abe frowned as he watched the woodcutter leave, and said, mostly to himself,

"There is always an appeal for justice—if only to heaven."

Chapter 19

A be was out of sorts and jumpy when he returned to his aunt's house, full buckets heavy in his hands. The raven sitting again in the tree outside the front door did little to relieve either feeling. At least Aunt Rosanna was out visiting with a friend, and would not make some comment holding him personally responsible for the bird's behavior. He felt no better at noticing through the window that it was still there when he had finished his morning chores.

After answering a soft knock at the door and selling a dozen eggs to a regular customer—a self-assured little girl who had introduced herself as "Louise, but everyone calls me Lulu even though I hate it"—Abe sat at the kitchen table to practice reading from the latest lesson that Gershom had set him to.

He'd mastered the letters, and learned to pick his way through the strange combinations—Gershom called them 'digraphs'—as well as the vowel combinations that Gershom called 'diphthongs,' and he found it actually exciting to be able to make intelligent guesses as to how the words he used every day might be written down.

His handwriting, too, had begun to occasionally meet with Gershom's approval, and the lesson to which he had set Abe was to read and then copy out in his finest hand was the first full passage in the primer. The first line, though, as he worked it out, drew him up short. "I will fear God and honour the King." Was it possible to honor a King who would empower such officers as the self-dealing governor and his surveyors? By all accounts, no report of misdeeds of any Crown officer had brought action from the King.

Was not the question of honor one that, in some sense, went both ways? He wished that Gershom were here to discuss the matter with, as the tutor was both open-minded and clever in explaining the conclusions that he had reached, while leaving open the possibility that Abe would come to have a different opinion, without it being evidence on its own of a flaw in either Abe's thinking or his own.

He shook his head and copied the line out, his writing painstaking, and the scratch of his pen against the paper halting and uncertain. When he was writing an example for Abe, Gershom's pen sounded rhythmic and smooth, punctuated with decisive strokes and the sharp retort of his dotted letters and periods. Abe knew in his heart that he would eventually reach the same level of proficiency, but he knew, too, that it would be the work of many years of practice.

The next line was hardly better, and indeed it brought tears to Abe's eyes for the first time in months over the losses he had suffered. "I will honour my Father & Mother." With neither remaining to honor, or even to disobey or disappoint, what meaning could a statement of duty like this have in his life? He felt certain that he had honored them both in life, though he supposed that he could do more to honor them in death.

The graveyard remained a place of such awful memories that he had avoided it entirely ever since the second burial there. He made a sudden decision to go to the gravesite and see the place where his father and mother rested, and to find out whether there was any honor to be gained in spending time in their company. His aunt had been making hints about his duty to go to the grave site, and he suspected that she would be thrilled that he had taken her up on those hints at last.

He set aside his lessons and dressed again for the cold outside. He knew that he'd be able to find the gravesite—Aunt Rosanna had griped to him about the incredible expense of the simple stone she'd had placed for them—and he could hardly think that the inherent dread chill of the place would have any effect one way or another on him in the cold winter air.

Opening the door, Abe could feel no effect of the full sun of the day on the temperature outside. The raven still waited for him, uttering a welcoming croak and shrug when it spotted him. Feeling whimsical for a moment despite the dark thoughts that drove him out of the house, Abe croaked and shrugged back at the bird. The raven blinked at him, its black eyes revealing no hint of its thoughts.

Abe went through the front gate, closing it carefully behind him, and turned toward the graveyard. The raven hopped down from its perch in the tree and stood on the fence, calling to Abe as though encouraging him. The bird's interest in Abe, which would have mere months ago caused him to break into a nervous run, now barely raised his eyebrows.

Some of the churned-up mud of the road had thawed in the bright sun, even if the air felt no warmer. Abe found himself stepping to the edge of the road to avoid the muddy center, which he knew would cake filth onto his shoes, requiring long and careful cleaning when he got home.

The snow had a thin crust over the top of it, and he liked the sound of it crunching under his shoes as he walked. Turning off the road, he wasn't surprised to see that there were few footprints in the snow leading to the gate and into the graveyard. He was surprised to see that there was somebody else already there, laying what looked like pine boughs on a stone.

It was Betty who turned around and saw him standing by the gate. She lifted one of the boughs and smiled sadly. "Evergreen, don't you know? Even if my parents could not last forever, at least I can keep a symbol of life near them always."

Abe nodded in acknowledgement and made his way through the tidy rows of gravestones to where his parents' stone stood. He studied it, noticing that it was plainer than many of the ornate stones around it, standing starkly upright with crisp, pure snow drifted slightly about it. He realized that with his lessons from Gershom, he could now pick out the letters forming their names, engraved in the thin slab of plain fieldstone.

Cyrus Sawyer—it occurred to him to wonder at the strangeness of the letters that had come to spell that name—and under it, simply the numbers 1732 and 1771, separated by a dash that seemed barely sufficient to capture the life and ambition that had spanned those years. Beside his name, Abitha Sawyer, 1734-1771. That she had been a dedicated mother and wife, a skilled cook, even with inadequate provisions and tools, and a gentle soul, all of that was left off the simple stone marker.

There was a verse carved into the rock above their names, and with some effort, he sounded it out. "Death is a debt/"—the last word of that line took him some time to work out—"To Nature due/That I have paid/And so must you." The sentiment sounded ery much to him like something that Aunt Rosanna would like, nd at which his father would have scoffed, if he deigned to give it ny response at all.

Cyrus Sawyer did not believe in owing any debt that was ot sealed with a handshake or a contract, and as for reminding isitors that they would join him in the cold ground soon enough, hat seemed entirely out of character. He'd been more interested in he next opportunity than in high sentiments or the long view.

Abitha Sawyer, her name engraved for all time beside her usband's, might have liked the verse better. It reflected the sort f gentle melancholy with which she had accepted her illness and ecline. From the first moment she had coughed up blood, Abe had een her shoulders slumped and her back bent under the load of her nevitable approaching mortality.

Abe stood, contemplating the stone, and wondering what he point of coming out here had been, anyway. He had seen the eadstone before, and the presence of his parent's corpses under he soil, rock, and snow was neither novel nor comforting. Finally aving the knowledge to be able to make out the writing on the one was, he supposed, a decent reason for coming out into the old winter day.

As his eyes again traced out the letters representing his arents, he felt a touch on his shoulder, and he was surprised to find etty beside him, and even more surprised to realize that his face as wet with tears. Without giving the matter any thought, he ut an arm around the girl's waist, and she leaned into his shoulder. Neither spoke for a long time.

Eventually she broke the silence of the graveyard. "I like to ome out and just remind myself that there once was a time when my parents walked the earth, and cared for me, and did their best by me. I like to remember that I was not always alone in this world with only my goats and the raven for company."

Abe let her words hang in the air for a moment, and then answered, "This is my first time coming here since the day when my father was put to rest." He felt, rather than saw, her answering nod. With Betty leaning into him, an escaped tendril of her hair tickling his cheek, the prospect of paying the debt that his parents' stone proclaimed was owed to nature seemed more distant and less appealing than ever.

She shifted slightly under his arm, her free hand came up to his cheek, her fingertips cold against his skin, and she was looking into his eyes, her gaze steady and thoughtful. Then, as though it were the most natural thing in all the time since the world was young, her lips were on his, warm and soft, the contrast with the cold air and their dread surroundings so marked that it took his breath away.

Chapter 20

Abe looked over a forest of stumps where the swampy lot had been. The bitter cold that had set in over the fortnight since he'd visited the graveyard had ensured that the open water and swampy ground in the lot had remained solid enough for the woodcutters to work unimpeded. He wished that his path forward were as clear.

Aunt Rosanna had been almost pleasant, so satisfied was she at his progress in his lessons with Gershom. She'd only tsked to herself when Abe had relayed the news about the mast trees at the mill, though her frown had revealed deeper worry. Abe had opted not to say anything to her about the moment he and Betty had shared over his parents' grave. It had been over so quickly, as Betty pulled away and hurried out of the graveyard, pausing only to smile enigmatically at him, that Abe had suffered moments of doubting that it had happened at all.

And yet he could not shake the memory of the warmth of her breath on his cheek as her lips had brushed his and then paused. Each time he thought of it, he felt as though his stomach did a somersault against his heart. Had she reconsidered her claim that she had no interest in him? Was she simply toying with him for her own entertainment? Or was it just a moment of shared emotion finding expression in a kiss?

He wished that his mother were available to discuss the

whole situation with. He knew that his father would have been hardly any less mercenary than Aunt Rosanna, but his mother would have understood the roiled emotions that churned about in his heart. He realized that despite having the relative advantages of family who could take him in and provide a roof and meals for him, he was hardly any less alone in the world than was Betty.

He was left to think through all of these matters by himself, without anyone more experienced to tell him where he might have erred, or where he was failing to see the larger picture. He tried to be rational about the questions that posed themselves, unbidden, in his mind, but he kept coming back to the memory of that golden moment.

He shook himself and tried to focus on the task at hand. He needed to examine the work of the woodcutters and determine whether they had stayed within the lot prescribed in the contract, and also whether they had completed the work called for in the contract. It appeared that the boundaries had been observed faithfully, the trees outside of the lot left unmolested, and those within felled with as much of their timber as possible removed for delivery on sledges to the mills.

A fresh snowfall, squeaky underfoot in the frigid air, had covered the traces of where the trees had been removed, and made it difficult to judge whether the ground litter had been removed and piled for burning as required. There were immense piles of the trimmed-off boughs of the trees set about the lot, ready for burning in more favorable weather, and the sight of the loose pine boughs reminded Abe yet again of the whole chain of events in the graveyard.

Satisfied that he had verified the execution of the contract as well as could be done at the moment, he decided to go back to his father's house to warm up and eat a bite of dinner. He decided that he would go out to the old grove of mast trees after he'd finished eating to see whether their serene presence might help him to clear his mind and understand what he ought do next.

His aunt had sent him out this time with a small packet of rashers of bacon, as well as the inevitable eggs. He hoped that the eggs had not frozen again—they were quite inconvenient to cook in that state—and that the bacon was fresher than it had been the last time she had sent him out to cook for himself. He was relatively certain that it was not supposed to have a green cast to it, and without the chickens to toss it to, that slab of bacon had gone entirely to waste.

The cabin was dark and cold, and his fingers were numb as he worked to produce a spark from his tinder kit to start up a fire in the hearth. He blew through his hands to try to warm them, but succeeded only in making them damp, which chilled them further. Finally, a long yellow spark flew from the flint and steel and into the prepared tinder he'd laid. Shortly, he had a pleasant, crackling companion in the cabin, and though he knew it was silly, he felt less alone than he had when he'd walked in.

The eggs felt as though they had stayed warm enough in his knapsack, and the bacon looked and smelled fresh. His aunt had tucked a hoarded apple into the bag as a surprise, and he grinned as he took a bite of it. In short order, he was spitting the seeds into the fire, with the bacon popping merrily in the spider.

He pulled the rashers out onto his plate when they were crisp enough for his taste and cracked the eggs into the grease in the pan. They popped and splashed, causing small flares of bright flame where the grease landed on the hot coals below. The bacon wasn't really cool enough to eat, but that didn't keep him from nibbling at a corner that hung out over the edge of his plate as the eggs cooked. He chewed thoughtfully, humming to himself as he flipped the eggs.

His mind drifted back to the comfortable and warm feeling of Betty's head on his shoulder as they'd stood together. As exciting as the kiss afterward had been, he thought that just standing together like that, sharing the experience of spending time honoring and remembering their lost parents, might have been the more important part of the day.

Once he'd eaten and cleaned up after himself, Abe decided it was time to go and seek the peace and silence of his favorite grove of mast trees. He hoped that their presence would help quiet his thoughts enough to start making sense of the day.

Outside, a breeze had sprung up, making the already cold air feel even colder yet. He pulled his cloak tighter around himself and was glad for the warm clothes that Aunt Rosanna had provided for him. The familiar path from the house to the grove was marked only by the prints of squirrels and other small animals that had blazed the trail long before he had started using it.

In one spot, the crust of the snow was broken through with the tracks of what he thought might be a catamount, but there were too many other prints in a confusion around them for him to be sure. Farther along, he thought he could discern the tracks of a deer as it wandered through the woods, looking for shoots to pull up through the snow.

He had always enjoyed trying to identify the different animals that had passed this way by their tracks and marks in the snow. He'd learned to recognize some from his father, a couple from his mother, and a large number by simply seeing the animals in question as they left their traces. He was not inclined to trap animals, nor did the hunt hold any attraction to him, but he appreciated knowing what was going on in the woods around him.

Another animal pathway joined the one he was following, and he was surprised to note that there were human footprints mixed in with the animal. As far has he knew, he was the only person who'd discovered the grove, other than the surveyor who had cut the King's mark into the mast trees around its perimeter.

The footprints looked fresh, and wondering whether the person who had made the tracks was still about, he quickened his pace. When he reached the quiet grove of giants, though, he was disappointed to see that whoever had left the prints appeared to have paused here themselves, leaving a circle of well-trodden snow in the middle of the grove, but had then left, going deeper into the woods.

Abe was both intrigued and relieved. He wanted this place to be one where he could go to be alone, and not a place where he'd have to worry about meeting any other soul. At the same time, it was interesting to him that another track led someone to the spot, and even more curious that the trail led deeper into the woods after the other person had left the spot.

He took a deep breath and crouched down against the steadying trunk of one of the trees, consciously trying to push the matter out of his mind so that he could focus on the troubles that had driven him here in the first place. The snow and cold masked most of the familiar scents of the place—the sharp aroma of pine, the warm and fertile smell of the dirt underfoot, and the occasional reek of some animal that had marked its territory. In place of these familiar smells was the crisp cleanliness of the winter air, which chilled his nostrils.

There was no sound but the sighing of the wind through the tops of the trees far overhead, and the rhythmic, slow creak of the trunks of the trees around him. A clump of snow slipped from a bough somewhere far above him, falling with a dull whump of impact into the snow at the base of the trees.

Aunt Rosanna had told him that she would never accept Abe involving himself with Betty, that her prospects made her an unsuitable match to someone in his position in colonial society. The prospect of being a grant holder and a man of means ought to have broadened his choices, he thought, but she seemed to believe that it ought to constrain them.

He and Betty had a great deal in common, and it was clear that despite her claim that she had no designs on him, she found something in him appealing enough to want to turn to him for mutual comfort in a moment of high emotion. He knew nothing of how or when she had lost her parents, and he found that he suddenly had a keen interest in the details of that.

For his part, though he truly had not thought about pursuing a match with anyone, he could see the advantages in having a confidante with whom he could discuss matters of importance in his life-someone other than his snappish aunt. And, of course, Betty was terribly pleasant to stand beside and wrap his arm around. Further, although Betty was determinedly odd, he believed that she was entirely trustworthy—and he could not say the same about his aunt.

That bag of money still haunted him, though he had not

asked her about it or admitted that he even knew about it. Too, although she said that she had only his best interests at heart, Abe felt pretty certain that if it came to it, she would see to her own comfort before his.

Finally, the very idea that she was better equipped to select a partner for him—a spouse when it came to that—than he might be himself was absurd on the face of it. If she was so qualified to make an appropriate match for him, well, where was her appropriate match for herself? Abe actually chuckled aloud at the realization of how ridiculous the idea ultimately was.

While he might owe her a debt of gratitude for arranging for the lessons with Gershom and seeing that he was properly fed and attired, that did not extend to permitting her to manage every detail of his life. Some things, he thought as he stood and started back to the warmth of his father's cabin, a man needed to do for himself.

Chapter 21

Abe and Aunt Rosanna were just sitting down to a meal of salt beef soup when there was an urgent rapping at the door. Abe looked at his aunt inquiringly, and she shrugged. "Go and see who disturbs our meal," she said, waving him toward the front door.

He opened the door to find the chief of the woodcutter crew on the step, holding his hat in his hands and looking agitated. Behind him, the man's horse was haphazardly tied to the tree by the front gate. Abe asked him, "What is it?"

The man's words tumbled out in a rush. "The magistrate's gone and summoned the mill owners to face charges in Portsmouth next week. We're raising a subscription to hire a lawyer to represent them, and we wanted to ask your contribution to the expenses."

"Bid him enter," Aunt Rosanna called from the adjoining room. "Calvin can join us for supper if he must, but I'll not have your soup grow cold while he demands money we can ill afford for a matter that is not our doing."

Abe stood aside and waved the man in, frowning at the mud that he could see clinging to his boots. That would be a job to clean up, later that evening.

The man followed Abe into the kitchen, and Aunt Rosanna asked, "Will you join us for soup? It's nothing fancy, as we're not great cooks, but it'll warm you and give your belly something to work on."

"Nay, I cannot stay, but I appreciate your thoughtful hospitality. The mill owners—"

"I heard your appeal," she snapped, interrupting the man. "Now explain to me how this is any concern of ours?"

The woodcutter raised his index finger for emphasis. "It actually should concern you gravely. Should the magistrate press the sawmill owners to learn the source of the timber they took in violation of the King's Wood, and if the men haven't the representation of an experienced lawyer, they might feel that they could best preserve themselves by saying what they know . . . " He trailed off delicately.

Aunt Rosanna pursed her lips tightly for a moment before answering, and Abe could see that they were white with her rage. Finally she spoke, her voice shaking in anger. "Do you mean to sit at my table and threaten blackmail against me, unless I should pay for a lawyer to defend and advise men who ought to have been circumspect enough to have avoided being found out in the first place?"

"Nay, nay, not at all." The man pushed himself away from the table, his hands raised placatingly before him. He seemed genuinely taken aback at the suggestion that he was trying to extract money by threats.

"I am only trying to explain to you that you are not so uninvolved in the matter as you may imagine. Men who are compelled under oath to speak the truth, and compelled by other means to speak the full truth, or even to speak what truths they imagine their questioners may want to hear, without the benefit of advice from expert counsel, well, they may utter things that could bring ruin upon even innocent parties."

Aunt Rosanna's mouth settled into a grim line, tensing when he said the word "innocent."

The man continued, "In any event, I am not here to demand the whole sum of what will be needed to hire counsel for them, but only to ask you to add a share to the amount."

Aunt Rosanna's voice was like the rap of an axe against heartwood. "How much?"

"Three and a half crowns." It sounded from his tone as if for this part, at least, the man felt on solid ground.

Aunt Rosanna fixed him with a glare that had more iron than warmth. "And what is your share in the cost of this defense?"

"'Tis also twelve shillings sixpence," the man said steadily. "Though my share in the proceeds from the timber is less, my risk at the hands of the magistrate is greater."

Abe was surprised to find that his aunt was looking to him for his opinion. "It comes out of your inheritance; what is your mind?"

He blinked away his surprise and gave voice to his thoughts. "'Twas our timber that got the mill owners into trouble, so it seems only just that the proceeds from our timber ought help to try to get them out of trouble."

At last, she nodded crisply. "Fine," she said, adding, "But the boy goes with you, so that he can bear witness to the case."

Abe's head snapped up and he looked at his aunt with disbelief. "What of my lessons?"

"You can take your primer and Gershom can set you to some exercises for as long as you're gone."

"And my chores?" Abe was feeling a growing sense of both

ear and excitement at the prospect of going to the capital city. It vasn't London, but he'd never been to Portsmouth. He supposed hat his father must have gone there when he received his land grant, ut he'd never said anything about it.

"I was able to do those for myself before you arrived, and I an get them done by myself in your absence." She turned back to he woodcutter. "When do you ride for Portsmouth?"

"In the morning, if I should have the amount of the ubscription in hand."

She nodded. "You shall have it, and your horse can carry he boy that far with you."

"Yes, ma'am. Thank you, ma'am."

She frowned in reply. "You've delayed us in our meal so that ur soup has gone cold. Leave us; I'll have the boy and your money eady in the morning."

Immediately after dinner, Aunt Rosanna sent Abe to go speak vith Gershom, who congratulated his student on the opportunity o travel, and jotted down a few exercises for the journey. Still ncertain about undertaking travel with a near-stranger, Abe had alf-hoped that the tutor would send word back to Aunt Rosanna hat his lessons should not be interrupted. He resigned himself to he inevitable when that possibility had been extinguished.

Trying to sleep that night, his good clothes and primer lready packed in a rucksack at the base of his bed, Abe couldn't elp but think that he wished he'd been able to ask Betty what she hought, or at least tell her that he was going to be gone.

He'd have some new stories to share with her when e returned, but he hoped that she wouldn't worry that he was voiding her. They had spoken just a couple of times since their chance meeting in the graveyard, and he was disappointed that she hadn't brought up their meeting, as well as relieved that she hadn't brought it up. On balance, he was satisfied to leave the moment as just an unspoken connection between them.

They had discussed the weather—fresh snow each time, as it happened—and the welfare of her goats and the chickens she had purchased. The goats were, as usual, pretty self-sufficient, even in the depths of winter, though they steadfastly refused to eat snow while they could rely on her to bring them warm water.

The chickens were weathering the winter in the yard of the house where she had her room, and the landlady had taken a liking to them, so that even when Betty was away with the goats, she ensured that they had fresh scratch and water.

"The clever little things found a place to lay where my landlady would not miss seeing the eggs—right on her front porch, just outside her door," Betty had said, laughing. "She stepped on them the first time, but ever since, she's been able to gather them for me. Of course, I share with her, anyway."

Her raven had been around pretty frequently, though, to his amusement and Aunt Rosanna's continued irritation. He'd wake up, look out the window to his room and wave to the bird before heading downstairs to do his morning chores. By the time he went out the door, the bird was usually waiting for him in the tree in the front yard, and it greeted him with a shrugging croak before flying off to the rest of its business for the day.

Abe fell asleep thinking that if the raven were able to actually communicate with Betty, he could at least be sure that she would learn that he had left the village on horseback, headed to Portsmouth.

Chapter 22

A be rode in thoughtful silence behind Calvin on his horse, their pace only a bit better than they would have made on foot. The horse could not be induced to go faster, but Calvin seemed unconcerned, so long as they arrived in Portsmouth before week's end, when the lawyer they had engaged needed to be paid.

In addition to the money that she had given to the woodcutter, Aunt Rosanna had pressed a handful of coins into Abe's hand, "for your expenses along the way." She had instructed him minutely on the etiquette of the traveler that morning while they waited for Calvin to arrive. Abe only hoped that he would be able to remember it all.

"When you go to a tavern and inquire after a room, you must be sure to ask for one that is away from the dining room, if you wish to get any rest at all in the night. I have heard stories of men drinking and making bawd right up until the cock's crow in the morning. You will need to keep your wits about you, which will mean that you must be well-rested."

Abe had rolled his eyes, after making sure that she had her back turned to him. Did she really think that he would have to engage his own room? He expected that Calvin would handle the details of their accommodations and food, as he would their route.

"You must doff your hat and bow courteously to your

betters once you are in the city," she said, picking up a new thread of thought. "You may have the opportunity to meet many men of influence, and to make your impression upon them. That impression will be a lasting one, for good or for ill, so take care that they think well of you on parting."

"Yes, ma'am." Abe had gone from feeling like he was being dispatched on important, adult business, to feeling like a little boy all over again.

"And another thing, the women in the city cannot be trusted—" a knock at the door stopped her, and she motioned to him impatiently to go and answer it. Abe had never been so glad to have an interruption, and greeted the wood cutter with more enthusiasm than was strictly proper.

Calvin was in a curt mood. "You have your bag? And you, the money we agreed on?"

"Aye," said Abe, while Aunt Rosanna dourly held up a bag that clinked softly as Calvin took it from her.

He nodded approvingly. "Specie is always more welcome than notes. If the lawyer offers us a discount for it, I will be sure to return the appropriate amount to you."

"See that you do," Aunt Rosanna said crisply.

Calvin mounted the horse with a practiced step up into his stirrup, the far leg swinging smoothly into place. Once he was settled on the horse's back, he pulled his foot out of the stirrup and pointed to it. "Foot here," he said to Abe, who stepped up and lifted his foot into the loop as indicated.

The woodcutter reached down to Abe. "Up you come, my young friend."

Abe grasped the man's hand firmly and pulled himself up

behind the wood cutter, as though he'd been doing it all his life. A moment later, though, he was flailing and grabbing Calvin's shoulder to keep from sliding over the far side of the horse.

Although Calvin kept his place on the horse and Abe recovered his balance, Aunt Rosanna had to muffle her laughter. Despite his annoyance at having looked the fool, Abe had to wonder at the sight of his aunt laughing—he wasn't sure that he had ever seen that happen before.

Her expression returned to a grim look of concern. "Travel with care," she said. "And you," she said, catching Calvin's eye, "Be on the lookout for footpads. These are unsettled times, and desperate men will turn to desperate measures."

"Missus Sawyer, I've heard naught of any highwaymen in these parts, neither this season nor any other I can recall. We will be fine, and so will your money." Abe couldn't see the man's expression from where he sat, but he could see his aunt's reaction, and he was glad that they were departing.

"We'll be back in a fortnight or so, and I hope to be able to give you the joy of our victory in court. The lawyer we have engaged is said to be the best available in all the colony."

She favored the woodcutter with a dour frown.

"In this colony, under this governor, I have no faith that justice is even available to ordinary people, no matter their means. A fine lawyer is no bulwark against the petty self-dealing of the King's men in these parts."

The wood cutter leaned down in his saddle to speak to Aunt Rosanna in an undertone, and Abe shifted his seat to keep himself balanced. "You ought be mindful of who might overhear you giving voice to such sentiments. It is one thing to disparage the laws of the Crown's grants; it is quite another, more dangerous thing to disparage the King's men themselves."

Aunt Rosanna rolled her eyes. "They are but men, not gods, but your warning is well-taken. I will keep my opinions of them to myself, but see that you take my words to heart."

"Aye, ma'am, I shall." The wood cutter had urged the horse forward, and the last that Abe saw of his aunt, she was turning around to go back into the house out of the cold air. Her head was shaking slightly as it did when she disapproved of something that Abe was doing, but not enough to correct him.

As soon as they were out of earshot, Calvin said to Abe, "She's a right terror, isn't she?"

Abe shrugged. "She means well, I'm sure. She is trying to do right by her brother's legacy, while maintaining what she can of her own life, despite my unlooked-for arrival into it. She is fixed in her ways, for certain, but she's not as bad as all that."

"If you say so, but she was very difficult when we were trying to work out the details of our contract for the woodlots. And then, the business of insisting that the written contract say one thing about the mast trees, while our verbal instructions were quite different. I acknowledge fully that she took her advantage in that matter. If it comes to it, what's on paper leaves me and my crew to twist, while she walks away without a word on the page to connect her to those trees."

They crossed onto a wooden bridge just then, which spared Abe the necessity of responding for a moment as the reports of the horse's hooves on the deck of the bridge made speech impossible. The planks of the bridge were slick and icy, and Calvin slowed their pace even further until they were on the far side, giving Abe a hance to consider his answer.

"She negotiates hard, I know, but I trust that she is fair in
elivering what is promised, once you do come to an agreement?"

"Aye, that much she is." Calvin fell silent at that point, and
eemed to be willing to let the matter drop. Abe focused on taking
1 the scenery, as this was the furthest he'd been from home since
he day he was born. The road, such as it was, wound over and
round the hilly terrain. Deep forest lay on both sides, punctuated
vith clearings or trails down to homes from time to time.

Despite the early hour of the day and clear skies overhead, so
1uch of the light was swallowed up by the trees towering overhead
1at it felt more like late afternoon. The chill in the air that persisted
·om the overnight cold made Abe's breath puff out in clouds before
is face, and he adjusted his muffler to better protect his face.

They came to a crossroads, and Calvin confidently directed
1e horse to the right, leading them onto a somewhat more
stablished looking road. At least the mud here was less frozen, and
1e trees did not crowd so closely overhead.

As they rode along, there were more and more areas where
1e trees on either side of the road had been reduced to stumps,
aving great swathes of cleared land, and opening wide, snow-
overed vistas out over the countryside.

Abe leaned forward so that Calvin could hear him. "It
oks as though my father's grant is not the only one that has been
·orked in these parts of late."

Calvin nodded. "Aye, though my boys and I have had
aught to do with this work. These lots are part of the grant that
enning Wentworth gave to old Mister Josiah. The old man doesn't
ardly come out to these parts, but he sends his wood cutters to

get as much wood off the land as he can. They say that the old man gave the governor's uncle some favor or other, and was richly rewarded for doing so."

Abe frowned. "Does the history of corruption go back so far, and the King has done nothing about it?"

"Aye. Mister Josiah has the second-biggest holdings in this area, and he's never come and worked a single honest acre of them. Now, the Randalls, whose grants backed up to some of your father's, those two worked their land as hard as anyone I've ever known. It's a real pity what happened to them, though."

Abe had never heard his parents speak of the Randalls, which seemed odd if their land adjoined his father's. Of course, his father was scarcely interested in the doings of any of their neighbors in the village, so Abe reflected, he supposed that it wasn't that much of a surprise that he'd never spoken of them.

Abe shook his head. "I've not heard of the Randalls."

Calvin tsked to himself and answered, "I'm not surprised. They made their home in the part of their grants nearer to the river, and spent most of their time there. But they were the biggest landholders in the area, and as I said, they worked every day of their lives to secure and improve their grants. They cleared off the land, raised up stone walls, and built a tidy little house on it."

He nodded for emphasis. "Fortune seemed to smile on whatever they set their hands to. Their timber was all exempt from the King's mark, which made clearing the land as easy as you could like. The land they cleared and fenced was well-founded, fertile, and they had good luck in what they chose to plant and raise."

Abe could see the edge of Calvin's frown as he continued, "However, it seemed that fortune was just toying with them.

They had improved their house to make more room for their two children, but something went wrong with the flue in the second fireplace they put in."

He shook his head sadly. "When the house caught fire, the only one to get out was their daughter. The husband and wife, and their little son, all died in the fire. It still brings a tear to my eye to think of it."

"That is awful," Abe agreed, horrified.

"Their daughter has been a little off, a little different ever since, as you might expect. She moved away from where her parents' home was, and someone in town took her in until she was able to take a room of her own." Calvin twisted in the saddle to look at Abe. "I'm a little surprised that you hadn't heard of it prior to this. After all, I believe that you know the girl—she's the one who keeps goats on her parents' old grants, and consorts with a raven about town, and I've heard it said that you and she are friends of one sort or another."

Chapter 23

A be's head was still reeling as they arrived at the tavern where Calvin said that they would rest for the night. Betty, heir to the biggest landholdings in the area? If this was true, then why did Aunt Rosanna suspect her of trying to find her fortune in ensnaring him? Why, if anything, the converse was true—he would increase his own fortune were he to combine it with hers.

It did not seem possible that his aunt was ignorant of Betty's history. She seemed to know far too much about everything that happened around the town for that to be the case. Of course, a newly-arrived young woman, appearing one day without a family in the village was likely to be of less interest to Aunt Rosanna than it had turned out to be to Abe.

However, Aunt Rosanna seemed to be keenly aware of who had—and hadn't—fortunes she considered worthy to consider joining to his. It seemed impossible to Abe that she was completely ignorant of the girl's family holdings. Why, then, did she have such disdain for Betty?

Calvin interrupted his chain of thought. "Come, let us see about rooms for ourselves." He dismounted and held out a hand to Abe to help him down. Abe slid off the side of the horse and found that his legs were nearly numb from the effort of riding all day. He had been aware that he was developing bruises in unfamiliar places, but as sensation returned to his legs, they were cramped badly enough that it was hard for him to walk.

Calvin laughed at his wide-legged stance. "You'll get used to it, my friend. Follow me inside, so that I can talk to the tavern keeper." Inside the tavern, it was warm and aromatic with the smell of fresh bread just coming out of the oven. Abe inhaled appreciatively as he unwrapped his muffler, and Calvin laughed again. "We'll sup soon enough."

He approached the tavern keeper and held a brief, quiet conversation with the man. He slid a couple of coins across the table to the tavern keeper and motioned to Abe to follow them. The tavern keeper led them up narrow, creaky stairs to a room with low ceilings—lower even than Abe's room at Aunt Rosanna's house—but with a window looking out onto the cluster of houses along the road that they had taken into town.

A small bed stood against each of the two walls, separated by a small table under the window. Calvin nodded to the tavern keeper. "This will do. Can we sup now, or are you still preparing the day's meal?"

"Nay, it is ready. It is nothing fine, just some bread and a plate of boiled beans. If you need more, it can be arranged, for an extra charge."

"I expect that it will suffice. I'll bring my horse around to the stable boy, and I'll be in directly." He turned to Abe. "Go ahead and start without me. I won't be but a minute."

Seated at the long table downstairs with several other travelers, Abe was pleased to find that the food was more plentiful than the tavern keeper's words had led him to expect, though he realized quickly that he could make beans better himself. The bread, though, was quite good. He and Aunt Rosanna either did without or traded with a neighbor for eggs, so any bread was a treat.

The texture was coarser than the neighbor's bread, but the flavor was about the same, the rye and corn blending in a rich, dense loaf. Calvin came in as Abe was chasing the last of the beans out of his bowl with the dark crust of his bread.

He sat down, and the tavern girl brought him his plate. He leaned forward and said to Abe, "That accursed stable boy demanded separate payment, and I had to send for the tavern keeper to set him straight. Then, I felt it prudent to observe him stabling my horse, else he might take out his frustration with me on the poor beast."

He sighed. "What is it these days, that everyone seems to be more interested in doing what is good for his own pocket, rather than doing what is right? When I was that boy's age, it was impressed upon me that a man provided honest value for what he was paid, and would never seek to cheat a customer."

He scooped up a bite of beans on a ragged piece of the bread that he'd torn off. Chewing thoughtfully, he nodded. "At least the tavern keeper himself seems to be an honest man." He raised his hand to get the attention of the tavern girl, who came over, her head bowed modestly.

"Can my friend and I get some cider, perhaps?"

"Of course, sir. Ha'penny a cup, if you please."

"Certainly." He dug into his pocket and tossed a copper coin to the girl. "Keep the rest for yourself."

She protested, holding the tuppence out for him to take back. "Oh, nay, sir, I am not that kind of girl."

Calvin smiled ruefully, shaking his head. "I meant no

offense. I merely sought to supplement your wage with a gift, with no expectation that you owed me anything beyond swift service and a pleasant demeanor."

The girl pocketed the coin, smiling. "That I can offer you, sir, with a clear conscience."

As she walked away, Calvin shook his head again. "Do you see what I mean? People assume the worst of each other these days, instead of starting from a belief in the basic goodness of their fellow man."

Abe said nothing, as it seemed that the more experienced man wasn't looking for a real answer, but wanted only to give voice to his frustrations. The girl returned with a smile and two mugs of cider, and Calvin nodded his gratitude as she walked away.

He lifted his mug to Abe. "Here's to a journey well begun and to success at the far end."

Abe lifted his own, touched it to Calvin's, and drank deeply. He missed cider, having had it only a few times while his parents were alive, and not at all now that he lived with Aunt Rosanna. His aunt had lectured him on the dangers of any form of strong drink, and while she particularly scorned those who drank whiskey or rum, she did not exclude cider from her household prohibitions.

Abe drained his cup, earning him a smile from Calvin. "I think I'll go on up to sleep," he told the older man. "Though I but sat behind you on the saddle all day, I find that I am as tired as I have ever been."

"First time on a horseback journey will do that to you," Calvin said, understanding. "I'll try not to disturb you when I come to bed myself."

Abe made his way up the stairs, his legs protesting every

step. It seemed that sitting at the table had been enough for them to stiffen up. In the room, he slipped off his boots and laid down on one of the beds, not even bothering to undress.

He awoke to the sound of the latch rattling and Calvin throwing himself onto the other bed. The man's arrival had interrupted a pleasant dream, and Abe struggled to return to it.

He had been in the grove of trees near his father's cabin and the day had been warm and sunny, though the light that filtered through the trees was pleasantly muted. As he'd stood in a sunbeam that pierced the canopy of pine boughs overhead, the sun's warmth suffusing him with calm, he'd heard his mother's voice.

"You're going to be just fine, son. You're doing fine." She'd never called him "son" in life—always "Abe," or "Abimeal" if he was in trouble—but just the memory of the sound of her voice had given him comfort.

As he sank back into the dream, he realized that he wasn't alone in the grove. Betty was with him, smiling at him as though she knew something that he didn't. She whirled around in the clearing at the center of the grove, her skirts flying out about her ankles, and she laughed.

Calvin groaned and rolled over, and the noise of his bed creaking was enough to shatter the dream entirely, no matter how hard Abe tried to return to it.

Chapter 24

"There's Portsmouth," Calvin said as they topped a rise in the road. Below them lay a broad bay and on the far side, a tidy-looking settlement crowded around the shores of a low-lying peninsula. A number of small boats and a couple of larger ships stood at anchor, though the view was obscured by an island in the bay. The sight caused Abe's stomach to give an unpleasant lurch.

Abe frowned. "I don't guess that your horse will swim that."

Calvin laughed. "No, no, we won't ask him to attempt it, either. We'll wait for the ferry to the far side. We could take the road to the west and cross at a bridge up there, but we're in a hurry today, so the ferry will save us a day's travel."

"That makes more sense. Uh, Calvin, I have never been aboard any kind of a boat before. I am embarrassed to admit it, but the prospect gives me a fright."

Calvin turned around more fully to look at Abe and assess whether he was serious or not. Abe felt certain that the fear he felt was reflected on his face, for Calvin nodded and turned back to face the bay. "'Tis nothing to be afraid of, my friend. The ferry crosses probably six times a day, both ways, and has done so for years without incident that I've heard of. Why, there it is now, floating along like a leaf on the water."

"Nay, I understand that as a matter of intellect," Abe said. "But the thought of traveling over water, though I know full well that people do it all the time, it just seems unnatural to me. If I step into water, my foot goes straight to the bottom. When I have gotten into a pond, I sink. I understand that a leaf may float upon water, but a horse is a heavier thing, never mind a horse and two men on a boat that weighs as much as a house."

"Yet you confess that you know that the thing is done, every day."

"Aye. I can see with my own eyes that there are boats of various sizes afloat right there." He gestured toward the quays alongside the city below. "I can see the thing, without fully believing that it is possible. Even without belief, I can admit that it happens anyway."

"So what is the problem, then?"

"My gut still tells me that it makes no sense, that it should not work, and that boarding that ferry will end only in us sinking to the bottom of that bay."

Calvin turned and favored Abe with a sour look. "We're not going around. I cannot afford the time. Can you close your eyes and merely tell yourself that the horse has adopted a strange gait for the time it takes us to cross?"

Abe sighed heavily. "I can try."

Calvin grinned. "That's a good lad. Let's get down there before the ferry arrives, that we may be on the next crossing."

Abe was no more certain about the ferry when he saw it at closer range. The ferryman had one eye covered with a dirty strip of cloth, and his face around the patch was a mass of old scars. Abe tried not to stare, but it was difficult, to say the least.

"You may as well come down off the horse, give the poor beast a break," the ferryman said to Abe and Calvin.

Calvin smiled at the man and handed over the money for their passage. "Thanks, we prefer to remain mounted. Been riding since the sun rose this morning, and we're both pretty stiffened up."

"Suit yourself," the ferryman said and turned away, grumbling under his breath. "You try to offer some fair advice, but do they listen? Nay, they'll keep their own counsel, follow their own way. There's no use in even trying, is there?"

Abe looked around and asked, "Are we afloat now?"

Calvin stifled a smile. "Aye, the ferry doesn't come up on land to load and unload. As soon as we set foot on the deck, we were afloat."

For some reason, the knowledge that they were doing the thing that his gut had told him was impossible helped to steady Abe's nerves—more than had any intellectual knowledge that people did it all the time.

Rather than closing his eyes to endure the passage, he found himself looking around in anticipation of the trip. When another couple of passengers arrived, on foot and on horseback, the ferryman evidently judged it worth his while to make the crossing again. He cast off from the shore, raising a small sail to catch the breeze coming in from the mouth of the bay.

Although the ferryman looked deeply bored at the whole operation, it was a completely new experience for Abe. He observed with close attention all of the ropes that the ferryman worked to control the push of the wind on the ferry, and the action of his hand on the rudder, steering the small vessel.

The air smelled different here than anything Abe had experienced before as well. There was an unpleasant hint of decomposing fish, of course, as well as other off-smells, but overall, the air here smelled sweeter and fresher somehow to Abe than it did back inland at his father's grants.

As they hove close to the quay at Portsmouth, the foul odors began to dominate again. Abe supposed that it was due to fish and other creatures of the sea washing ashore more frequently, but he admitted to himself that this was not an entirely reasonable assumption—some must have come from the great city itself.

The ferryman steered toward his normal landing, calling out, "Hold onto something solid, for we'll be stopping pretty sharp-like in a moment." He was as good as his word, as the ferry came to an abrupt halt as it ran up ashore a bit. The ferryman let down the planks at the prow of the vessel, and Calvin clucked to the horse to urge it forward.

Portsmouth was, Abe could see, like nothing he had ever experienced before. There was practically no room between the close-packed houses and many shops. Abe marveled at the strange sight of shops specializing in just one sort of goods. The roads were cobbled, making the weary footfalls of Calvin's horse sound sharp and energetic as they echoed.

More than that, there were people everywhere Abe looked. In the village, it wasn't uncommon to encounter someone on their way to the well or to the mercantile, but here, it looked like it was unavoidable. There were men in tricornes and boldly-colored jackets with gold buttons, and women in mob caps and tightly-laced bodices, their modesty at risk as they lifted their skirts to avoid the slushy snow at the margins of the road, exposing low shoes and even a flash of a stocking-clad ankle.

Also shocking to Abe was the degree to which the people here seemed to be strangers to one another. Instead of the friendly greetings—or at least tolerant acknowledgements—exchanged by the people he knew when they encountered one another on the road, these people seemed to brush past each other, and around Calvin's horse, without even making eye contact, much less exchanging social pleasantries.

Most were on foot, though there were a few other horses around, and even a carriage ahead of them down the street. The majority of the structures along the water had two, even three stories, and there were a couple made of brick, a strange sight indeed to Abe's eyes. Most of the buildings he had ever seen were constructed of wood, though a few older houses were made of stone—usually stone that had been pulled from a field to enable a plow to pass through it.

Calvin guided the horse around to a side street, where the buildings were a bit more modest in size, and there was actually room to walk between them. There, he reined the exhausted animal to a halt, patting it on the neck. "Here's where we'll stay for a few days, while the lawyer prepares and argues the mill owners' cases. Come, let us go inside and secure a room."

The now-familiar routine followed: greeting yet another tavern keeper, Calvin negotiating with him, and being led to their room. Abe pulled his boots off and unwrapped his muffler, and then fell to the bed Calvin had pointed him to. "I could sleep here for a fortnight," he declared, and Calvin laughed.

"Well, don't sleep for more than an hour or so right now, else you'll miss your supper. I'm going to go and find my friend who fronted the money for the lawyer and inform him that we have raised funds sufficient to repay him for the lawyer's fee. I'll see you downstairs after that."

"Sounds good," said Abe, his eyes already half-closed. His legs ached from days of riding, and he was afraid to investigate the saddle sores that he thought would make it nearly impossible to sit for dinner anyway. He was glad to hear that they would be staying in Portsmouth for a few days at least, so that he would have time to heal up and stop aching.

The allure of traveling, or at least the degree to which Gershom had made it sound alluring, seemed very distant to Abe at this point. He was grateful to be able to get some rest, and he fell into a deep, dreamless sleep that was interrupted only when Calvin banged into the room.

"That scoundrel of a lawyer took his fee, argued the case, and then turned around and accepted a commission from Governor Wentworth to be the deputy surveyor of the King's woods! We've been taken for fools, and the corruption of the Crown's name continues unabated."

Chapter 25

Over supper, Calvin continued to fulminate. "Oh, he made a grand bargain for the mill owners. They need only pay their fines—which I suppose will help to line his own pockets, as well as the governor's—and the governor will suffer to let them keep the timber for which they have already paid, and the lumber that they have already cut. Isn't that just so benevolent of the governor?"

Abe chewed the stringy meat from his bowl, only able to nod sympathetically.

Calvin was undeterred by his lack of conversational involvement though. "And as for the lawyer, he is keeping our fee, saying that he negotiated a reasonable settlement, avoiding a warrant for the mill owners' arrest, so long as they render unto Caesar, as demanded, under a law that is unjust and arbitrary, and which is enforced only for the personal benefit of the governor and his cohorts."

Abe swallowed with some difficulty, following the food with a healthy gulp of cider. "Is there no appeal to a higher authority, no redress?"

"Nay, not as a practical matter. If the mill owners cannot re-take possession of the logs before they have been spoiled by the damp and bugs, they will have no value to anyone, and a formal complaint to the Crown or to Parliament would take so long to arrive and be answered that it is just the same as there being no recourse at all."

"Isn't there something the mill owners can do?"

"Aye, they can pay, and give the governor what he demands, or they can defy him, and test whether he has the will to swear out warrants against them. Executing those warrants will be quite another thing, too, as the woods are deep, and the governor's authority ends at the frontier to Massachusetts or New-York."

Abe stifled a gasp. "Would the mill owners go so far as to openly defy the governor's order and flee his authority?"

"Aye, particularly when that authority does not appear to be in keeping with good propriety."

A gruff-looking man further down the table leaned over and interjected, "Even when the good governor is fully within his authority, the people are of a mind these days to answer him with open defiance. Had you heard about the excitement over the brig *Resolution*?"

Calvin answered carefully, "Nay, we are not from these parts. What of it?"

The stranger grunted and said, "Aye, I had gathered that. A few months back, a Yankee brig arrived from Saint Martin's, in the Indies, carrying a load of molasses hid in its hold. They declared and paid their duties on the rest of their cargo, but with the duty on French molasses being so dear, the ship's master had determined to smuggle it ashore."

Abe exclaimed, "But that would be defrauding the King himself!"

The stranger shrugged. "The King is far away, and the duty is steeper than is just. Nor have the King or Parliament ever consulted with any representative of the people here as to whether they desired to pay such a duty." He snorted. "The plain fact is that the duty was imposed not so much to put money in the King's purse as to give advantage to the plantations on the British Indies over their French neighbors."

Calvin spoke up. "Thus raising the cost of rum production in Massachusetts, and the price of rum everywhere." He grinned. "'Tis no good way to encourage compliance."

"Aye, there was quite a stir about it when it was imposed. Couple of years later, the Parliament quietly reduced the duty, but it still rankles, and it's still worth circumventing whenever a ship's master thinks he can get away with it."

The stranger smiled grimly. "The master of the *Resolution* was not so fortunate. The King's men inspected and found the molasses in his hold—'Tis nearly impossible to hide a hundred hogsheads—and they seized up the ship and put a seal on the molasses. The whole lot of the cargo and the ship alike would then have needed to be transported to Halifax, where the Vice-Admiralty court would condemn it and sell it to satisfy the claims against it."

"The master could lose his ship for smuggling?" Abe was shocked at the severity of the punishment.

"Aye, but this time, some men disguised themselves and took up clubs to chase off the customs officers and took the molasses off the ship. The governor offered a reward of two hundred Spanish dollars for anyone willing to turn Crown's witness and bring the perpetrators to justice."

Calvin whistled. "'Tis a princely sum," he said.

"Aye, but none was tempted by it, and both the molasses and those what took it remain on the wind. The molasses has doubtless been reduced to rum by this time, and the men, well"—he winked—"there remains no evidence by which to convict them, even if anyone with knowledge of their identities were inclined to do so."

Abe said, "'Tis a shocking picture of riot and disorder that you draw, sir. Are many matters settled thus, here in Portsmouth?"

"Nay," the man replied, "not so many, but my reason for speaking up was merely to give you hope that the corruption of the government does not go without answer. The governor may tighten the vise as he likes, but in so doing, he gives courage to those who have cause to resist. There is only so much that a man can take, after all, and this government seems determined to test those limits."

He scowled. "It's gotten to where an honest smuggler can scarcely ply his trade anymore, between the customs house and the accursed *guarda costa* set upon the waters hereabouts by the King's navy."

Abe frowned. "The 'guard of cost?'"

The man uttered a bitter, sharp bark of laughter. "Nay, the coastal guard. They patrol and seize as prizes all sorts of merchants whose only sin is in seeking to supply the markets on these shores without the interference of the Parliament's duties and regulations. But yes, they do 'guard costs,' making everything more expensive."

He sat back upright and raised his mug. "I apologize for inserting myself into your conversation, as I said, but take heart that your friends' legal troubles may find an answer outside of the courts that is more satisfactory than the one they've found inside."

Calvin raised his mug in answer. "I thank you for that, sir.

'Tis a dangerous thing, to discuss such matters in a place where your words may be overheard, and your sentiments mistaken. I salute your boldness, sir, and wish you all safety in these fractious times."

The stranger nodded acknowledgement and turned his attention to his meal. Abe leaned across the table toward Calvin. "Do you really think that matters will come to such a pass?"

"Nay," Calvin said, his expression hard. "The mill owners will line up like good little sheep to pay their fines. There's not a one of them with the backbone to give the governor a fight, and their mills are too fixed a target for them to pick up and flee the governor's justice."

Abe nodded. "And the lawyer, who took our money and then turned his coat against us?"

Calvin turned his head and spat on the floor, eliciting an angry glare from the tavern keeper. "I'll not speak aloud what I'd like to do for him, should I encounter him in an alley after dark. I've heard it said that there's not a lawyer in the land who can be trusted as far as he'd slide on an icy road, but this is my first personal encounter with the species."

He grimaced. "They seem more interested in how they can twist the law to the benefit of the highest bidder than in actually ensuring the administration of justice."

"And there is naught we can do, it sounds like," Abe said, frowning.

"Nay, save pray for that meeting in an alley . . . and I doubt that a man smart enough to bargain for an appointment by the governor will venture into any place where he is not secure for some time to come. He must know that he has earned the permanent hatred of every man who hired him for the purpose of delivering them from the governor's sudden enthusiasm for the King's woods."

"But being a Crown officer gives him some protection, does it not?"

"Aye, the officers of the Crown seem to have their own separate system of justice. They work alongside the magistrates, who answer to the same authority as they do, and there is no incentive for the magistrates to impose any real justice on them, should they commit some violation." Calvin sighed.

Abe leaned forward even closer and lowered his voice. "Are we not approaching a breaking point of some sort, if justice is denied at every turn? The Crown's officers massacre our people on the street in Boston, and are held blameless. They seize the trees we were purportedly granted, and then demand a ransom for their return. They patrol the waters off our shores, not for our protection against foreign threats, but for the purpose of interrupting our trade. Where does it stop? How does it stop, if not in violence?"

Calvin looked grim. "We are but a disorganized collection of colonies, and the King has whole armies that he can set to the business of subduing us, if he so chooses. Further, he has been raising militias on these shores, presumably for our defense against the French and the Spanish, but in fact, it would be all too easy for the guns trained outward to be turned around in an instant to face us. There is no remedy for the ills that currently visit these lands but to let the heavens deliver their inevitable justice on the works of man."

He looked around, then added with a half-smile, "Of course, that doesn't mean that we shouldn't give God a little helping hand in delivering justice, while we wait."

Chapter 26

As Calvin had been paying for their rooms and meals, Abe had not had to spend any of the money that Aunt Rosanna had provided him. He knew that the coins in his purse, along with the money paid to the faithless lawyer, had come out of either the earnings from the timber or else what his father had set aside, so by the right of inheritance, it was his money.

With nothing better to do, and money in his purse, he told Calvin that he was going to go and have a look at the town and see what the shops had to offer. Calvin, still slumbering after a long night of drinking cider and rum, groaned and rolled over, shielding his eyes from the light that streamed through their high window.

Abe left him to sleep, closing the door quietly behind himself. Outside, it was snowing lightly, which made walking a bit treacherous, particularly once he reached the cobble-paved streets in the center of town. There'd been little to look at on the side street where their tavern was located—primarily what looked like private residences of varying levels of prosperity—but once he reached the paved street, he found it lined with shops of many sorts.

One sold only a dizzying array of meat, hung in the open window for the inspection of passers-by. A boy sat on a stool under the awning of the shop, and as quickly as Abe wondered what he was doing there, the boy leapt into the air, yelling and gesturing at a bird that had tried to land on a hanging leg of pork. The bird changed course and flew off to land on a nearby tree, where it perched, watching the boy and the meat intently.

Abe shook his head and walked on, passing a shop that bore a sign covered in closely-spaced print. Abe stopped and sounded it out, seeing that it claimed that the shop was the best in the colony for exotic spices and the finest tea. Abe was tempted to step inside, as the morning tea at the tavern had been most unsatisfactory, but as he could not think of a way to steep tea in his room, and he expected to be leaving in a matter of days anyway, it didn't seem worth it to lay in a stock for that purpose. He made a mental note of the place, though, to check and see whether its prices were better than the mercantile back home.

The tea shop gave way to a haberdashery, clothes hung on display in the window, which did not interest Abe particularly, as his aunt had gotten him into new clothes just after he'd moved in. As he passed the millinery next door to it, whose sign simply depicted a hat, he took his own hat off and examined it. It was functional, but he wondered whether a new hat would charm Betty . . . or make her think that he was putting on airs. He decided not to take the chance and kept walking.

An entire shop devoted to books drew his attention, and mindful of his primer, sitting up in the room above the tavern, he decided to go inside. The proprietor sat behind his counter, reading, and he looked up when Abe walked in. Giving Abe a courteous nod, the man said, "Good day to you, sir. In from the country, I take it?"

Abe frowned. "What makes you say that, sir?"

The bookseller smiled. "You walk like you've been on horseback for days, and your clothes are clearly designed to be

sturdy, rather than making sacrifices for fashionable ostentation."
He motioned self-deprecatingly at the ruffle on the front on his
own shirt.

Abe smiled in reply. "You aren't wrong about my having
spent entirely too long on the back of a horse of late. Indeed, if it is
not too great an imposition, I might ask your advice for somewhere
to seek a salve for the worst of my suffering from that ride."

The bookseller laughed aloud. "Certainly, sir, and my
compliments to you for being so forthright. Most of the dandies I
see in here would hem and haw about what they actually wanted
for the space of half an hour or longer. The apothecary just four
doors down will be able to give you a salve that will sooth what
ails you."

He smiled broadly, and Abe smiled in reply, feeling abashed
at having been so forthright, despite the other man's praise for it.
The bookseller said, "That is not what brought you through my
doors, though, I wager. What sort of book might interest you? I've
a wide selection brought in from London, as well as a selection of
pamphlets and almanacs from Boston and Philadelphia, and a few
things from New-York and Charles-Town, and some items from
our local printers, too."

"In truth, sir, I am but learning to read." He spotted the
familiar cover of his primer on the shelf behind the bookseller and
pointed at it. "My aunt secured a copy of that one, there, for me,
and I am working with a tutor to master it."

"Ah, very good, very good indeed! I am always glad to see
a new reader come through my door, as he is almost certainly going
to become a great customer in the future. That primer is one of the
best, and I don't mind telling you that I sell more copies of it than I

do of any of the alternatives to it."

"I am happy to hear it, sir, though I must confess that I find it a terribly dour work."

"Well, aye, and it ought be—the point of reading is to improve yourself, is it not?"

"I suppose," said Abe with a tinge of skepticism audible in his tone. "But what I came in here for was to see whether there might be anything that I could purchase as a present for my tutor, by way of expressing my gratitude to him for his patience in delivering his lessons to me."

"Ah, a noble intention indeed! I presume that he is a learned fellow?"

"Aye, and he reads both the Latin and Greek, from what he has mentioned to me in the course of my lessons."

"Oh, that is simply marvelous. I have very little on hand in those languages, and what I do have, he has likely already a familiarity with. Has he an interest in the most current of news? If you are to return home soon, I can offer you the latest copies of the *Gazette*, printed in this very town, at four pence per issue."

"Aye, I am to return soon, and I believe that I can afford that expense." Abe thought for a moment. "If you have them, may I purchase the most recent four issues?"

"Certainly, my young friend. That will come to a shilling and four, and I'll fetch them for you."

Abe dug the coins from his purse and laid them on the counter. He swallowed hard at the total, but reassured himself that Gershom would treasure the gift. While he didn't know what arrangements Aunt Rosanna had made with the tutor, he felt certain that fresh reading material would be a more welcome compensation than mere money.

The bookseller returned to the counter with the newspapers, which he folded and presented gravely to Abe. "I thank you for stopping in today, sir, and I look forward to seeing you many times in the future. The apothecary is the one painted white, just past the yellow shop, up that way." He pointed in the direction that Abe had been walking already.

"Thank you for the directions, and I look forward to returning in the future as well," Abe said, and bowed in farewell. He slipped the newspapers into his haversack and went outside, pulling the door closed behind himself. The snow was falling now with more enthusiasm, and Abe decided to go directly to the apothecary, and then return to the tavern, so as not to be caught in an outright storm.

He walked through the slush at the boundary of the cobbles, counting the shops carefully as he went. While he felt relatively confident that he could work out the words written on a sign on the apothecary, he'd get there faster by simply following the instructions offered by the bookseller.

Although he'd managed to forget for a while where he was rubbed raw by the ride to Portsmouth, he was keenly aware of it as he went to go and find a cure, and he found himself walking stiffly, which made moving through the snow even more difficult.

The shop painted white also had a sign hung that depicted a mortar and pestle, which Abe took to indicate that the proprietor could blend what cures might be needed on the spot. He pushed the door open and closed it behind himself, finding that the shop was ill-lit, with small windows half covered in heavy draperies.

He ventured to call into the half-darkness as his eyes

adjusted, "Is there someone here?"

"Aye . . . aye . . . have some patience, boy." Abe could hear the proprietor moving around, and his voice sounded as though he were ancient. When his eyes could better penetrate the darkness, he saw the man moving from his comfortable-looking seat behind the counter to come up and greet him.

Standing up as straight as he could, the wizened old man gripped a cane tightly in one hand. "What brings you in here on a snowy day, boy?"

Abe took a deep breath and said, "I've just come on an extended ride on horseback, my first, and I have suffered some embarrassing wounds from the saddle and the roads."

The old man grinned, revealing a number of missing teeth, and cackled, "Oh, I reckon you have indeed. 'Tis the bane of every traveler who has not a great deal of experience to help toughen the skin. Wait here, and I'll prepare you a salve that will help your sores to heal."

As the old man moved about, pulling open tiny drawers and removing various ingredients from them, he called out to Abe, "How soon must you travel again?"

"I expect that I'll be returning home within the week," he answered.

The old man grunted and shook his head. "You'll just tear the wounds open again; I'd best make you a double dose, so that you can patch yourself back up when you get home. Better if you could wait until you've healed up completely before you travel again, but at least we can prepare you for the trouble to come."

"I do appreciate that, sir."

"Say nothing of it. Now be quiet for a bit while I get this

mixed together." Abe complied, and watched the man grind together ingredients, then mix them into a greasy base of some sort.

He scooped the mixture into a clay pot and then beckoned Abe over to the counter. As he drew near, Abe caught a whiff of the salve and recoiled. It reeked of sharp herbs and rancid fat, overlaid with the sweet odor of mint.

"Now, this is going to smart like all get out when you put it on, but presently, it will stop hurting. You may bind up the wound then, so as to avoid staining your clothing, and go on with your normal activities. You ought apply fresh salve every morning on rising, and every time that you will be riding, until the wounds have healed completely."

He set the lid onto the pot and gave it a quick twist to seal it into the wax around the rim, and then handed it over. "One and tuppence, if you like."

Abe frowned, skeptical that the salve would be so beneficial as to justify the expense, but not feeling that he could argue the point after the man had gone to all the trouble of making it for him. He dug through the coins remaining in his purse and handed over the price asked.

"Thankee kindly, good sir," the man said, sweeping the money off the counter and into his open hand. "'Tis a pleasure doing business with you, and I'll throw in some bandaging cloth for the payment in real money."

He turned away and dug around in a cabinet under the counter for a moment, grumbling as much to himself as to Abe. "Bills of credit everywhere, and all the guineas have flown back to England. There are Spanish milled dollars about, but most of my business doesn't rise to that level."

He sighed and placed a bundle of rags on the counter. "There you go. Just tear off the length you need, and you can burn it when you're done with it. Better that you burn it outdoors, if you can," he added sharply. "Might tend to flare up a bit in a fire."

Abe took the rags and wrapped the pot in them, then put the whole thing into his rucksack.

"Now, you'd best be going, as it's looking like it's ready to snow as hard as it did in that one storm last winter. That was a heck of a snow, though I suppose that you had much the same where you were, eh?"

"Yes, sir. As you said, I'd best be on my way."

"Safe—and comfortable—travels to you, my boy."

Abe found the snowfall intensified even more, with an appreciable accumulation on the roadway. There were but a few tracks in the new-fallen snow, as it appeared that most of the crowds he'd seen the day before had already taken to their homes and hearths. He headed directly back toward the tavern, despite the temptation to investigate some of the shops he'd bypassed on the way out.

Within a few minutes, he was back at the front door of the tavern, and inside he found Calvin sitting at a table, staring dully into a mug of cider. He looked up as Abe entered, and motioned the younger man over. "Sit, sit," he said, and waved down the tavern keeper. "Another cider for my friend, if you would."

The tavern keeper nodded and bent to pour the cider from a barrel braced under the counter. After he'd set the cider down in front of Abe and returned to his chair behind the counter, Calvin leaned forward and hissed, "Well, the other mill owners paid up, and have already been given leave to go and collect their illegal timber."

"And the men we sold our timber to?"

"Refused to pay. I hear that the governor will likely have the sheriff swear out a warrant against them before the day is out."

Chapter 27

Back in their room, Calvin started throwing his belongings into his rucksack. "'Tis best we be out of town before the warrants are sworn," he said to Abe.

Alarmed, the younger man asked, "Are we in some danger of being swept up in this matter?"

"Not much, but there is always the possibility that the governor will decide that he wants to make an example of a grant holder, and will press the mill owners for the identities of those from whom they secured the timber in the first place. Were that to take place, it would be mightily awkward for you or I to be present in the very seat of power."

"Aye," said Abe, and he began packing his few belongings as well. As he shoved his spare shirt into the rucksack, his knuckles bumped into the pot of salve still in the bottom of it. He cursed under his breath and continued packing. Gershom's newspapers he laid along one edge of the sack, in an attempt to keep them from being wrinkled or torn on the trip to come.

Calvin, seeing that Abe was nearly done, said over his shoulder as he left the room, "Dress for the storm, and I'll go see the ostler about getting the horse ready."

"Aye," Abe said, feeling a shiver of fright for the first time. It was one thing to face the remote possibility of being the target of legal action, but it was quite another to know that he was about to face whatever weather was building outside.

He peered out through the window into the darkening afternoon, where the snow still fell, but quietly, even gently, and not in a sudden rush as he'd sometimes seen it. The old apothecary had reminded him of the awful storm that had blown in from the Atlantic the prior winter. It had been in the course of that storm that his mother had first developed the cough that led to the consumption that had taken her life. While everyone had said that there was no way that the weather was to blame, Abe felt a thrill of dread pass over him at the prospect of exposing himself to another storm of unknown potential.

However, even as he was pondering these concerns, he was wrapping his cloak and muffler tightly around himself, so that when Calvin returned to the room, snow still melting in his hat, he was ready to follow the older man out of the tavern.

They left through the back door, where the ostler had Calvin's horse ready. "Yer a fool for traveling in this weather," the man said gruffly, but he handed over the reins to Calvin in exchange for a coin that flashed in the half-light of the alleyway. Calvin swung up into the saddle, then reached down for Abe's hand.

Now practiced, Abe swung up behind Calvin, wincing as he seated himself on the saddle. It would be a long evening of riding, no matter how far they got. "You say that the ferry won't be running in this weather?"

"Nay, he'll have gone home to wait it out, like any sane man would do."

"Very well, then, we'll find our way. Thank you for your concern and for the care you have given my horse. Until the next time I find myself in town, sir." Calvin tipped his hat to the ostler, who reflexively tipped his in reply, and then went back into the warmth of his barn, not even watching to see that the travelers got out of the alley.

Once on the road, Calvin directed the horse with confidence up the main street, and then onto another street that was paved, though their horse's hoof strokes were muffled in the accumulation on the surface of the road.

They went out of town on a different road than they'd taken by the ferry, and Abe occupied himself with memorizing every detail of he could drink in. Soon enough, the closely-spaced buildings of the town gave way to a few outlying farm houses, and then to open land and more forest. They'd long since left the cobbles for dirt, though it all looked the same under the blanket of fresh, scarcely-broken white snow.

As they rode, the snow seemed to be letting up a bit, and instead of becoming progressively darker, the skies actually lightened. Soon enough, Abe was no longer worried about the weather, as his attention was fully engaged by the ache of his saddle sores. He fervently wished that there had been some time to apply the salve before they'd had to leave.

By and by, the broad river came into view to their right, and as it began to narrow, Calvin pointed out an approaching bridge. They turned off the road to take the bridge, and Abe felt the other man relax a bit as they crossed over it. Though he knew that the sheriff could just as easily pursue them on one side of the river as on the other, should he be inclined to do so, it somehow felt safer to Abe to have the river and the bay between himself and the law.

The heavy snowfall had resumed falling thickly around them, and it muffled even the sound of the river under the bridge, as well as their horse's hoofbeats on the planks of the bridge. They reached the far side, and even those muffled reports became quieter on the dirt road.

"'Tis fortunate that I know the way," remarked Calvin. "A person could get lost in these conditions all too easily. We'll not travel very far today, as I wanted only to get out of the city."

"Aye," said Abe. "It looked like it was going to clear up there for a bit, but now it appears that we're in for a good bit of snow before it ends."

"I was hoping for an easier passage, but this suits our purposes well enough, too. There will be few others out on the roads, and none who can see us clearly, should we be pursued."

"Do you really think that we might be chased?"

Calvin shrugged. "I cannot be certain of course, but what sense is there in taking a chance, when the governor is clearly looking for chances to make examples of violators of the Pine Tree Law? The plain fact is that both you and I knowingly broke that law, and we are both subject to its sanctions."

He turned in the saddle to look Abe in the eye. "I don't relish either giving up half a year's income or more, or wasting away a year or more in a gaol in Portsmouth, for what is at heart an unjust law broken for just reason."

"I don't disagree, Calvin. I am just not accustomed to thinking about things as a fugitive."

Calvin chuckled. "Oh, we aren't fugitives until the sheriff swears out warrants against us, and before he did that, the governor would have to know of our roles in the crime. For the moment, we are but prudent."

Abe hardly felt reassured at this. Calvin's casual admission that he and Abe were both criminals set off a fresh chill of shock down Abe's spine.

They rode on in silence for a while, the half-light of the snowstorm slowly darkening as the afternoon wore on. Abe wasn't sure if he or the horse was more grateful when a public house loomed up out of the scarcely-relieved white swirl of the falling snow.

The sign bore a crude carving of a tree, and Abe could make out the words on it easily enough—it was the "Pine Tree Tavern"—and though his muffler was wrapped securely about him, the relentless snow had found its way down the nape of Abe's neck, so that he was eager to make his way out of the cold as quickly as possible.

Calvin pulled the horse up short before the door and dismounted into snow that was well up over the ankles of his boots, holding his hand out for Abe to help him down from the saddle. Sliding off the horse was a fresh agony, but it was driven from his mind by the even more discomforting feeling of snow filling his shoes. He exclaimed aloud, and lifted one foot from the snow in an attempt to keep it dry.

Calvin laughed and said, "Go on inside and bid the tavern keeper to come out and treat with me directly. Drink a flip as soon as one can be made for you; I will join you in a moment."

Abe went through the creaky front door of the tavern, into a blast of warmth and welcome. The tavern keeper leapt up from his stool behind the counter, saying, "You must be a determined traveler indeed to venture out in this weather!"

Abe explained, "Aye, and my companion awaits without. If you could go and speak with him first, I will wait here for your return."

"Certainly, certainly. Hang your cloak, take off your shoes, take a seat, and tell Prudence what you would like."

"Thank you, sir." Abe pulled his snow-covered outerwear and hung it up, then pulled his shoes off and dumped the snow out of them. He sat in the chair that the tavern keeper had indicated, and the waiting girl hurried toward him at her master's irritable wave. The tavern keeper, for his part, pulled his jacket and cloak on, and worked his feet into his boots, not bothering to lace them before he went outside.

"Good evening, sir," said the girl—Prudence, the tavern keeper had called her—"What is your pleasure tonight?" The girl was demure and soft-spoken, and Abe found himself involuntarily comparing her meek nature with Betty's self-assured eccentricity.

"My companion informs me that I ought have a flip, and that another one ought be prepared and held for his arrival, if possible."

"But of course," the girl said, and hurried back behind the counter. There, she poured ale into a pewter pitcher and cracked a pair of eggs into it—Abe admired her one-handed technique—and then topped it with a healthy tot of rum. She gave it a quick stir with a fork, and brought it over with her to the hearth.

She reached down to pull the flip dog from the fire, where it nearly glowed from the heat of the coals, and plunged it into the pitcher, where it sizzled and steamed prodigiously. She replaced the iron atop the coals, making flames leap up from the implement, and returned to the counter. She poured the drink from one pitcher to the other, her eyes focusing intently on the course of the frothy, steaming liquid through the air. Finally, she filled a mug from it, bringing it over to set before Abe with a flourish.

Abe nodded respectfully at the girl's impressive expertise at preparing the drink, and said, "Thank you kindly, Miss Prudence." She smiled prettily at him before ducking her head and blushing as she returned to her station behind the counter.

Calvin stomped into the tavern then, followed by the tavern keeper. They hung their cloaks and pulled off their boots, continuing their conversation from outside. "But you do still have a room?"

"Aye, though the sheriff and his deputy have the best rooms in the tavern, I do still have a smaller room adjoining that I can let you have."

"The sheriff?" Calvin's tone was sharp and Abe could hear the alarm that his companion was feeling as clearly as if he had clutched at his arm.

"Aye, he's out with a warrant for some scofflaws who he believes are somewhere in these parts. He is lodged with us until he finds them or determines that they have moved on."

Calvin released his breath gustily, and the tavern keeper asked suspiciously, "You aren't in some trouble with the law, are you?"

"Nay, nay, not at all. Well," Calvin seemed to decide to confide in the tavern keeper as he continued, "not at present, but I have been in the past, so I have an aversion to being involved in matters of the law if I can help it."

The tavern keeper looked at him, suspicion still etched on his scowl. "You will pay now, in that case. I've no need to be cheated by a man who has a history of disregard for the law."

Calvin looked for a moment as though he were going to put up an argument, but then his shoulders slumped, and he reached for his purse. "What is the price?"

After the business was taken care of, he sat down with Abe,

and Prudence brought over his flip. He wrapped his hands around it and shook his head, his mouth pursed in a sour expression. He said quietly to Abe, "Well, we certainly went to a lot of trouble to put ourselves right under the sheriff's nose, didn't we? And to be insulted by that cursed tavern keeper in the bargain."

He took a long pull at the flip and smacked his lips in satisfaction. "At least the tavern girl is good at her trade. I've not had a better made flip in years."

Abe didn't mention that he'd never had one before, but when he tried to emulate the older man's deep drink of it, he found himself choking and spluttering instead. His throat was on fire, and he remembered to his chagrin just how much rum Prudence had added to the drink.

Calvin was doing his best to suppress outright laughter, and finally managed to ask, "Have you never had strong drink before?"

Abe wiped his streaming eyes and answered evenly, "Nay, just the once at my father's funeral, which you may recall went no better for me. What betrayed my innocence?"

Just then, the tavern door banged open, and a group of men crowded into the room, the cold air blowing in behind them carrying the smell of rum and trouble. Abe noticed that their faces were all rubbed with soot, obscuring their identities, and a chill ran down his spine. One of them nodded at Calvin and said, "I didn't figure to see you here. Our business isn't with you, though."

He approached the tavern keeper, who huddled against the counter, shielding Prudence behind himself as the group of men surrounded him. "Tell us where to find the sheriff and his deputy, and this doesn't involve you any further."

Chapter 28

As the soot-faced men rushed upstairs in a mass to the room that the tavern keeper had told them was the sheriff's, their steps thundering through the building, Calvin and Abe looked at each other, their faces pale with shock and fear.

Abe ventured, in a low whisper, "You know these men?"

Calvin whispered back, "Nay, only the one, and him not so well. He was one of the mill owners to whom I sold timber from your grant, and one who had refused to pay the fines assessed by the governor. I had no inkling that he was prepared to take...direct action."

Upstairs, they heard the sound of someone pounding on a door, and shouted calls for the sheriff to show himself. Abe looked over and saw the tavern keeper comforting Prudence, who was openly weeping, while fearful tears streamed down his face as well.

Now they could hear the roars of the sheriff and his deputy as they were dragged from their room and confronted by the mob. "What business have you with us that permits you to drag us from our beds and hurl abuse at us?"

The growled answer was not audible from downstairs, but Abe and the others downstairs could clearly make out another voice calling out, "How many stripes do you reckon we should give 'em, boys? One for each stick they grabbed from us?"

The sounds of boots scuffling and the impact of a body thrown to the floor sounded on the ceiling, followed by shouted abuse and cries of pain. Then, "Hold him down, boys"—followed by the crack of a cane and an unearthly howl torn from the throat of one of the mob's victims.

Abe saw Calvin wincing at each stroke and its answering cry, and realized that he, too, was wincing in time to the sounds of the assault. There was another scuffle, and a series of thuds, and then a moment quiet.

One of the rioters must have been standing near the head of the stairs, for his voice could be heard clearly, saying, "I think they've had enough. Let's send them on their way." He was answered with a rumble of approval, and the sound of boots starting down the stairs.

The tavern keeper and his serving girl cowered back against the counter, and both Abe and Calvin looked down at the tabletop before them, neither venturing more than a glance up at the passing mob. Borne between them, Abe spotted a man whose clothes had been torn to ribbons, bloody flesh exposed beneath the scraps. His head lolled back, and Abe wondered if he was even still alive.

Another man was carried down the stairs, though the rioters slipped on the blood from their first victim and fell in a mass at the bottom of the stairs, laughing and cursing as they regained their feet and hoisted the second man back up.

After throwing both men out into the snow, one of their assailants came back inside. "Come and show us their horses," he commanded the tavern keeper, who followed reluctantly. In his absence, the serving girl slid down the wall to huddle in the corner where it met the counter. Through the half-open door, Abe heard rough laughter and shouts.

Through the window, Abe could see as the tavern keeper brought out two horses and was dismissed to return inside. There, the terrified man crouched down beside the serving girl, comforting her. Outside, there were hoarse jeers and crude suggestions shouted back and forth, as the rioters wrestled the two lawmen onto their horses and tied them in place.

Abe caught sight of a man using a knife to slice off the hair of a horse's tail. Then the animal shifted nervously, taking it out of his sight. "Cut it all off, and get the ears, too," one man called, and shortly afterward, Abe could hear the scream of a horse in pain, followed by more rough laughter.

The muffled hoofbeats of horses departing could be heard, and then there was silence, broken only by the sobs of the serving girl. A gust of wind blew the door open, and Abe rose wordlessly to go and latch it. Outside, he could see blood scattered crimson in the snow, along with hair from the manes and tails of the two targets' horses.

Small, dark shapes that he recognized with a gasp as four horse's ears were tossed at the entrance of the tavern, and Abe had to forcibly suppress the urge to be sick at the sight. He pulled the door closed and returned to his seat, shaking.

Calvin asked quietly, "They're gone?"

"Aye, but they..." Abe hesitated. "He cut off the ears and mane of their horses. Why on Earth would they do such a thing to the horses?"

Calvin shook his head, scowling. "It ruins the value of the animals, in addition to frightening them so that they'll run wild. The sheriff and his deputy will be lucky to survive, if they can't get control of their mounts pretty quickly."

Abe shuddered. "Did you have any knowledge that the mill owners were planning such violence?"

Calvin shook his head vehemently. "Nay, and had I known, I would have gone to the sheriff myself to warn him. While I had my concerns about encountering the man today, I bore him no personal ill will, and I certainly did not wish to see him come to grief."

He turned in his chair and called out to the tavern keeper, "Did they harm you at all?"

The man stood, helping his serving girl to her feet. He said something quietly to her, and she collapsed into a chair, looking vacant and stunned. "Nay, but what they did to the sheriff and his deputy was...dear God, it was nothing short of barbaric." He sounded shaken, and he went around the counter to pull a cup from underneath and filled it with rum.

After he'd drained the cup, he addressed Calvin, his eyes narrowed with suspicion. "Did you know those men? I heard one speak to you as though you were familiar to one another."

"Aye, I knew the one man, though his friends were not known to me. He is a mill owner, lately fined by the governor for possessing timber that violated the Mast Act. He failed to pay that fine, and I presume that the sheriff was here to arrest him."

The tavern keeper nodded, but his tone remained wary. "Some kind of chance it was, then, that you happened to arrive here and hear from me that the sheriff was in my rooms, just before the mob came to seize him up, eh?"

Calvin's mouth compressed into an angry, tight line. "Are you accusing me of being in league with those devils, sir? Or is the strong drink loosening your tongue and making you say things that you'll regret later?"

The tavern keeper stared belligerently at Calvin for a long moment, then looked away, shaking his head. "You're right, there's no evidence to connect you with that lot. Please accept my apologies...it has been a rough night for all of us." He looked at the trail of blood from the stairs to the door and remarked, in a lower tone, shaking his head sadly, "Rougher for some than for others."

Calvin nodded. "I do not fault you, sir. These are difficult days, and events such as this will only serve to make them more difficult yet."

"That is certain," answered the tavern keeper. "Everyone in this town will be suspect, in the eyes of the sheriff, assuming, of course, that he survives. I shouldn't wonder if the governor sends a larger force hence to apprehend those who took part in this riot."

Calvin looked up sharply. "Did *you* know any of them?"

The tavern keeper pursed his lips. "It is hard to say with certainty, the way they had blacked their faces, but there were a couple of them who I believe may have been from these parts. Should the question arise, I would be forced to give names."

"Has the governor even any such militia that he can call out for the purpose of putting down an insurrection? I know that some towns have drilled to hold their militias in readiness against the French or Spanish, should they decide to stir up troubles for the Crown again in these colonies, but would they truly be willing to turn out against their neighbors?"

"Oh, I think that they could be induced to do so," said the tavern keeper. "Put enough money in front of a man, and he's liable to do nearly anything you might like, and the governor has plenty enough money."

"It sounds as though we may none of us be safe here, then," Abe said suddenly. "Should the entire village flee before the governor acts?"

"That seems as though it might be a step too far," the tavern keeper said. "Certainly we should not rouse everyone in the night, against a possibility that won't come to pass before morning, if it should come to pass at all."

Calvin said, "Should the governor send his men hence, though, they will be in no mood to ask questions gently. After what was done to that sheriff and his deputy, they will be out for blood."

He stood and said, "As for the boy and I, we should be off now, as I've no doubt that the governor's men would want ungentle words with us, should they find us here. I'd take it as a kindness, were you not to mention to them that we were ever here."

Chapter 29

Abe woke with a start, sweat pouring down his face. He relaxed with the realization that he was back home in his own bed, with Aunt Rosanna's low, sloped ceiling close over his head, the sweltering heat of the top floor making him toss the blankets aside to cool down.

The sharp reek of the ointment prepared for him by the apothecary in Portsmouth rose to his senses, and he wrinkled his nose. Pulling his legs up slowly to his chest, he winced as the raw skin was stretched tight. He lowered them back down to lie flat.

He'd been dreaming that the rioters had caught up with him, and one had a knife to his ear . . . what would come next, he knew all too well, and he was grateful that he'd awakened before he'd experienced that part of the recurring nightmare again.

The rest of the trip home had been grueling, as Calvin had never really let them catch up from the sleepless night of travel in the snow that they had endured that first night, after they left the scene of the violence. Even when they had stopped at a tavern the following evening, Abe had slept fitfully, nightmares and the raw flesh of his thighs awakening him every hour or two throughout the night.

In his own bed, he had at least slept the night through, but he still realized that he was shaking in reaction to the nightmare. He took some deep breaths and glanced at the window to see how far progressed the morning twilight was. In the tree outside the window was Betty's raven, staring in at him. It saw him looking out and gave a quiet call of greeting, shuffling its wings over its back as though pleased with itself.

Abe nodded at the bird and decided to get up and get started with his morning chores. Aunt Rosanna had been greatly disappointed at the return they had gotten on her contribution to the lawyer's fee, but had insisted that he go to bed and rest, giving his sores a chance to heal. "I'll still expect you to complete your assigned tasks in the morning, mind you."

Downstairs, he found Aunt Rosanna already at the table, her tea in hand. "I should like to hear what transpired after you left Portsmouth from your own mouth, Abe. The partial report that Calvin gave sounded quite troubling."

Abe sat down, and she poured him a cup of tea as he laid out their abrupt departure from Portsmouth, the snowstorm that had overtaken them, and the events at the tavern.

"'Tis well that you and Calvin flew from that place, Abe. I have heard no news from those parts yet, but it seems impossible that the governor will not respond in some like fashion to the murder of his sheriff and deputy."

"They may still live, Aunt Rosanna," Abe had said.

"Regardless of whether they live, grievously scarred and marked for life, or have died, the governor will have to respond in kind, lest the people of this colony come to believe that they may defy him with violence and suffer no consequences."

"Do you know that this is not the first time that the people have defied the governor this season?"

"Nay, I had not heard of another incident."

"Just a moment," Abe pardoned himself from the table, and fetched his rucksack from upstairs. He pulled out the newspapers he had bought for Gershom and spread them flat on the table. "I have not yet had an opportunity to look at these and discover whether they might discuss the incident, but it seems likely."

Aunt Rosanna's eyebrow rose. "You bought these, and you are still working out words letter by letter?"

Abe frowned at her. "Aye, I bought them as a gift for Gershom, that he might be informed of events throughout the province, but I thought also to practice upon them, if you please."

Aunt Rosanna rolled her eyes, but kept her counsel. She joined him in scanning over the pages of the newspapers, until she said, "Ah, yes, this appears as though it may be the incident you're speaking of. May I?"

He relinquished the newspaper to her, and she read aloud, "'A Proclamation.' My, how official our governor gets, eh?"

She read, adopting a ridiculous heightened accent, "'Whereas I have this day received an Information or complaint exhibited by the Collector and Comptroller of his Majesty's Customs for the port of Piscataqua in the said province, setting forth that on the 26th October instant Richard Keating, Master and Commander of the Brigantine Resolution then in this Port came to his Majesty's custom house, and entered said vessel from Saint Lucia and Saint Martins, but did not enter one hundred hogsheads of molasses or thereabouts then on board with design to defraud the King of the duties due thereon.'"

She looked over the paper at Abe. "They thought they could hide one hundred hogsheads of molasses from the King's men?"

Abe shrugged in reply. "I don't know how large the vessel

is, nor how it might be laid out, but it sounds as though they were detected readily enough." Aunt Rosanna nodded, and she continued reading.

"'In consequence of which they seized said brigantine and the molasses then on board, agreeable to the laws, and put the officers belonging to the customs in possession of said vessel and goods to secure them, and that on the 29th instant between the hours of eleven and twelve o' clock at night, there entered on board said brigantine a numerous company of men in disguise armed with clubs, and wrested said vessel out of the hands of the proper officers then on board, turned some of them out of the vessel, and confined others in the cabin.'"

She set the paper down again. "Has nobody learned anything after the massacre at Boston and the unrest and riots that attended that event? How do they mean to preserve their dominion over these colonies, when men have shown that they will not hesitate to take such steps against them? How is it conducive to good order to so provoke our merchants and traders to the point where riot is their only option?" She sighed and picked up the paper.

"' . . . then proceeded to unload and carry away the molasses aforesaid. Wherefore they prayed that some method might be taken in order to discover and apprehend any of the rioters aforesaid that they may be dealt with agreeable to the laws in that case made and provided'"—Aunt Rosanna snorted, but continue reading.

"'I have therefore thought fit, by and with the advice of his Majesty's Council, to issue this proclamation hereby promising and engaging a reward of two hundred dollars'—two hundred dollars, why that's a year's earnings or more for most!—'to be paid out of the treasury of this Province to any person or persons who shall voluntarily inform of and discover any of the principal actors or abettors of the aforesaid illegal and riotous transaction, so that they may be convicted thereof, and in case such person or persons who shall inform as aforesaid shall be a party concerned therein except the principal, they shall hereby be exempted from any prosecution for the same. Given at the Council Chamber in Portsmouth on the 31st day of October,' et cetera, et cetera.''

She folded the paper back over and pushed it across the table back to Abe. "A whole lot of pretty talk, and I'll wager that nobody has come forward at all."

"Nay, not that I heard of," Abe confirmed. "Do you expect that the same will be the case with this riot at the tavern?"

She pursed her lips before answering. "As the sheriff and his deputy were assaulted, and one or both may have been killed, no, I don't think that the governor can afford to let this event pass without finding some appearance of justice against the rioters."

"Will they pursue Calvin and me, do you think?" He frowned at the thought of facing the sheriff—or his successor, if the worst had come to pass.

"I doubt it, but it might not be a bad idea for you to spend some time out of the village, against the possibility of pursuit. You are all too easy to find here in my home."

Abe looked up sharply at her. "Do you mean to say that I ought move back to my father's cabin?"

"Aye. In your absence, I had the opportunity to think about a number of things, and your composure after having been present to witness those terrible events in the night has confirmed what I was thinking."

Abe gave her a puzzled look and she nodded at him

emphatically. "You are becoming capable of managing your own affairs far more than I have been permitting you to do. It is time that you be given the opportunity to do so."

She stood and walked over to the cabinet, opening the door and pulling out a familiar leather sack. She set it on the table, where its contents clinked dully. Abe let his eyes widen a trifle, as though it were the first time he was seeing it.

"This is your father's fortune, saved for the day when he could return to England and establish himself. I discovered the place where he had secreted it shortly after his death, but until we got the inheritance straightened out, I did not want to share that information with anyone, against the possibility that someone might seek to claim that it was somehow not yours."

She motioned at the sack. "So, I put it away, and have used it for nothing. The money that Calvin delivered to me for this season's harvest is in here as well, less the contribution to that scoundrel of a lawyer. I paid Gershom and bought your clothing from here as well, but I've taken nothing for myself."

She tilted her head toward the window. "Between what I make from selling eggs and what my own father left for me, I have sufficient money to support myself in comfort enough."

Abe frowned and pushed the sack toward her. "I don't think I need this, at least not yet. So long as I can buy necessities out of the income from the woodlots, I should be fine out at the cabin."

Aunt Rosanna nodded. "I agree, and I'm heartened to see that you intend to be prudent with your inheritance." She stood again and put the sack back in the cabinet.

"It is probably for the best that you go out to the cabin today." She sat back down, looking at her hands on the table.

"Aye." He reached out to take them, saying, "I am grateful for all you've done for me. I will be back to see you often, at least to purchase eggs from you." He smiled. "I confess that I have become accustomed to having them morning, noon, and night, and it will be strange to go without."

She grinned back, perhaps the first true smile he'd ever seen on her face. "You'll not need to, my boy, as long as I've anything to say about it."

Chapter 30

It was a cold morning, and again Abe found himself breaking the ice away from the edge of the creek, so that he could dip out his morning water. Most of the winter's snow had thawed in the gentle warmth of the past fortnight, but the day had dawned clear and cold, and the grass underfoot had crunched loudly in the quiet of the morning as Abe walked out to the creek to fetch water.

As he repeated the familiar motions of gently submerging his dipper, to fill it without raising mud from the bottom, and then lifting the water into his pail, Abe found himself wishing that he were back in town, where even if he had to clear away ice in the bottom of the well, he could collect sufficient water for the day in just one or two buckets.

As he focused on the water swirling into his dipper again, a shadow passed over him. He glanced up to see Betty's raven landing on the far side of the creek. It peered at him with one shining black eye and then turned to regard him with the other eye, as though expecting to see something different.

"Good morning to you, friend," Abe murmured, and the bird croaked and shuffled its wings in reply. Abe returned his attention to the last dipper of water he'd need, and the raven hopped closer to the bank of the creek, apparently curious about what Abe was up to.

"It's all yours once I've finished," Abe said, and then shook his head at himself. He was becoming as barmy as Betty was, talking to the bird as though it could understand him. He stood and put the dipper full of water into his pail.

The raven launched itself across the creek and hopped over to where Abe had broken away the ice. It dipped its beak into the water and then raised it to let the water flow down its throat, repeating the motion a few times as Abe watched, a half-smile on his face. Perhaps the raven could understand him, after a fashion.

He stood, realizing with a pang that he missed encountering Betty in the village, even if it was an infrequent occurrence. He couldn't argue with his aunt's feeling that he was better off living out here in isolation for the time being, but without even his father for company, the old house was quiet and lonely. Comfortable though he was with his routine out here, he even missed his interactions with his aunt.

Of course, what the village could never give him was the serene security of the woods. As he stirred the hearth to uncover the prior evening's coals, still glowing and warm, he decided to visit his favorite copse of mast trees once he'd finished his lessons for the day. He fed some slivers of wood into the bed of coals, and laid larger kindling over it as it flared into life. As he cooked his simple breakfast, he thought about the progress he'd made in his reading and writing, and permitted himself a moment of pride.

Gershom had not yet been out to the cabin to visit him, though Aunt Rosanna had promised to dispatch him as soon as it was prudent to do so. Abe still had with him the newspapers that he had bought for his tutor, though. In addition to practicing copying out the pages that his tutor had assigned to him, Abe was laboriously working his way through the news articles and notices, using the exercise to hone both his reading and his handwriting.

He had set himself the task of copying out no less than one item every day, and on days where there was little else to do, he was sometimes able to complete an entire page before his hand cramped up to the point where he needed to stop.

Today, he had come to a page of notices, which ranged anywhere from the mundane—one shopkeeper begged the reader to consider the stock of finest-quality cloth, newly arrived from London—to the disquieting—a notice placed by a homemaker in town, seeking the return of her indentured servant, who had run off with the household silver.

Abe had filled a third sheet of paper with his careful, deliberate script, a faithful copy of the page, so far as he could tell, before he sat back in his chair and rubbed his stiffened hand. He smiled as he looked around his little cabin, content with his progress for the day.

Outside, the morning chill had given way to a sunny midday warmth that hinted at the promise of a green rebirth with the turning of the season. The woods were alive with the trill and chirp of birdsong, and he noted that the buds were starting to swell on the lilac bush his mother had told him was planted at the same time as Governor Wentworth's, before Abe was even born.

As he entered the sanctuary of the copse of mast trees, he saw at once that he was not the first there. Leaning against one of the trunks, almost as though she were listening to its sap rise, Betty smiled to see him.

"You have found my little place for contemplation," she said, grinning at Abe.

"Nay, 'Tis you who have discovered mine," Abe said. "I had always thought that this part of the woods lay on my father's grant."

She regarded him for a moment, delight still evident on her face. "Ah, it may be so," she said. "My childhood home once stood by the river, just on the other side of this ridge. When I was a very small girl, I had adventures all through these woods, without any regard for which bit belonged to whom."

She smiled more broadly again, adding, "I had no conception that you and I were neighbors all of these years. 'Tis curious, indeed, that we never met in these woods as children at play."

It was Abe's turn to smile at Betty as he said, "There's not much surprise in it, in truth. I was kept busy as a child with chores and work around the house. My father wasn't much for leaving a child time for play, and when I could slip away, I usually came only to here."

A thought dawned on him. "I have seen footprints coming here, this past winter, that looked like someone coming here for the same reason as I do. May I presume that was you?"

She nodded. "I have come out here a couple of times in the last few months, looking for advice that my raven could not offer without exposing his biases." She smiled, shaking her head. "He likes you, perhaps as much as I have come to, and so his counsel in questions about you is no longer impartial."

Abe wasn't quite sure which part of this extraordinary comment he ought to respond to first. After a moment, he chuckled and said, "You should probably know that these trees are unlikely to be impartial in my case, either, as they have known me far longer than has your raven." He smiled, and she laughed aloud in reply.

"The trees do not answer my questions, my dear friend. Their thoughts are far too slow for me to hear. No, I come here to see whether my mother might have any words for me. I cannot hear her at all in the graveyard, but here, I sometimes think that she visits me and offers me her advice when I ask it."

Abe shook his head, no longer wholly convinced that the girl was merely making sport of him, and instead beginning to wonder whether she was completely right in the head. He'd never heard her sound so sincere in her eccentricity before today. On the other hand, he had to admit that he'd readily enough accepted that the raven was her best friend, and not just a companionable animal.

She closed her eyes as a beam of sunlight found its way through the pine boughs overhead to illuminate her face, and then she spread her arms wide, spinning and laughing, her skirts flying high above her ankles. It seemed like the most familiar sight in the world to Abe, though he could not put his finger on why that might be.

She came to a giggling stop in front of him, a bit out of breath. A strand of hair had escaped from under her cap, and she grinned impishly at Abe, saying, "I don't know what came over me, but the sunlight and the warmth of the day are such a relief after this winter that we've had. Don't you find it so?"

She stepped toward him, her gaze unfaltering, so close that he could feel her breath tickling his cheek as she looked up at him. He found his voice and answered, stammering a bit, "A-aye, 'Tis a warm day."

She giggled and danced away, spinning again. Her cap fell off entirely this time, and she laughed as she bent down to retrieve it from the ground. "You must think me terribly improper," she teased. "I know for a fact that your aunt does."

Abe frowned. "What my aunt thinks is her own problem, not mine." He thought for a moment, and then added, "Nor need it be yours. In any event, I expect that her opinion of you is likely to shift dramatically when she learns that you are heir to an even larger land grant than am I. Furthermore . . ." He trailed off, suddenly unwilling to complete aloud the thought that had occurred to him.

She looked at him, smiling coquettishly. "Furthermore?"

"Nothing," he said, a touch more hurriedly than was absolutely necessary. He was still surprised at himself for the idea that his aunt's objections to Betty might disappear entirely at the prospect of joining the two grants together, should he and Betty . . . wed.

It was one thing to overcome Aunt Rosanna's flinty gaze that seemed to appear every time that the topic of his friendship with Betty arose, but to leap from that to . . . marriage? His thoughts were interrupted by Betty, whose tone had turned suspicious as she said, "How do you know of my inheritance, anyway? And what is it to you, other than more prime timber to be turned into lumber and a smashed landscape?"

"No, not at all—it merely serves to allay my aunt's suspicions that you are interested in my friendship somehow because I stand to gain an inheritance. I learned about your history as happenstance on my trip to Portsmouth. I knew not that my associate even spoke of you until he asked whether I knew you, after telling me the story of your family's loss."

"I see." Betty crossed her arms, looking at the ground pensively. "And what else did your friend say of me? Am I a laughingstock, whose story is passed around as a three days' wonder, and then I am but dismissed as cracked, or am I regarded as an object of pity, defined entirely by the tragedy in my past?"

Abe stepped forward and took Betty's chin in his hand, lifting her eyes to meet his. "Neither. You are seen as someone who has suffered losses beyond reckoning, and who has found a way to survive those losses, where a lesser person would have been destroyed by them. I admire you, Betty, for having created a life for yourself that doesn't rely on pity, though you could command it if you wanted."

He saw tears form in her eyes, and he released her chin, pulling her into an embrace. He murmured into her ear, "I respect you for having a strength in your circumstances that I know I do not have. You live with purpose, where I just do as I'm told. I hope to have a companion as wise as your bird is in the years ahead."

He released her from his embrace and held her at arm's length, again seeking out her eyes with his gaze. He was suddenly more certain of this than he had been of anything in his life. "I should like very much to have you as my companion, Betty, if you will have me."

Surprise registered in her expression. "Do you mean . . . ?"

"Aye. I mean to ask you to marry me, Betty." She flung herself back into his arms, saying nothing for so long that he began to wonder if he had leapt ahead too far, too fast.

Finally, she said, her voice strained, "I had begun to wonder if you would ever overcome your aunt and ask me. Of course I'll marry you. I've known I would ever since you carried me home in the snow, and saved my life, at some cost to my dignity. Yes, Abe, I will marry you."

Chapter 31

Aunt Rosanna was glad enough to see Abe again, though she chided him for not waiting until she had sent word that the affair at the Pine Tree Inn had blown over. "Just got word this morning that the sheriff and his deputy both are recovering their injuries, and the rioters have been named and called to answer to charges."

Abe sighed with relief at that, and then launched into a hurried explanation of the fact that he and Betty were in love, and wanted to marry at the earliest opportunity. The words spilled out of his mouth so quickly that he hardly paused to take a breath, never mind permitting his aunt a moment to interrupt him. He hurriedly added the information he had learned about the land grants that her father had held, pointing out that it was a convenient happenstance that they adjoined his own father's grants.

Although he'd expected that Betty's prospective inheritance would be enough to quiet Aunt Rosanna's objections, he had not anticipated the argument that she made. "You are both just so young, Abe. Why, neither of you is even of age yet, and it is hardly decent that you should be considering marriage without first having learned a little more of the world, and established yourself with a station in life where you can contemplate a family."

Abe grimaced, taken aback for a moment. "'Tis true that we are both of tender years, and yet she has had to make her own way in the world since the loss of her parents, and I have means enough at my disposal to ensure our financial well-being." He gestured behind where his aunt sat, at the cabinet where the leather purse was secreted.

"Furthermore, with our land holdings, we can lease out the cleared portions to tenant farmers, which will ensure a steady and dependable income, while maintaining the wooded parts as an assurance against any troubled times that may come to pass."

Aunt Rosanna grimaced over her tea cup and took a long, noisy sip from it. "You are still too innocent of the world, Abe, and she is hardly more than a child, herself." She raised a hand to quash his reply, which died on his lips as she continued.

"I will grant you that she has seen after herself already for longer than most who marry, and you are not wrong about your own means. Even so, I have some experience with the bitter fruit that may be harvested as the result of proposing marriage at too young an age."

Abe frowned, puzzled, and she continued, "I was no older than your Betty when I met a fine, gentlemanly lad and felt that my heart would simply burst to pieces if I could not be joined with him in marriage at the earliest possible date. Your grandmother forbade it, and though my Henry and I talked about elopement, his parents prevailed upon him to make a more sensible match, and in the end, I wound up alone."

Abe felt his jaw sag at the thought that Aunt Rosanna could ever have been so hot-blooded as to consider an elopement, but before he could muster a reply, she spoke again, a sad, distant look in her eyes. "Henry's father-in-law provided an ample dowry, which is more than my own father could offer, but Henry found no joy in his marriage, and when he failed at his apprenticeship, he joined the King's militia, and was sent to fight the French and their savage allies in New-York."

As surprising as the rest of the revelation had been, Abe was still more surprised to see that his aunt's eyes glistened with unshed tears as she concluded, "Henry never returned, as he took ill and was left in a hasty grave near the fort, far from his widow and I." She looked up at Abe. "She remarried, and her connections enabled your father to gain a generous grant from Governor Wentworth."

"Do you mean to tell me . . . " Abe was stunned into silence and could not complete his question.

Aunt Rosanna nodded though, and answered, "Yes, Abe. Henry's widow was your mother, and neither Henry nor I ever told her that we had once burned for one another. Instead, I watched her let him go off to his death, and then marry my own brother, since she had not taken enough from me already."

She drained her teacup, and Abe thought that she might at that moment be wishing that she had something stronger in the house. "Since I never married, and your father was already well-provided for, the money that my father had saved for my dowry came to me, along with the house, just a few years after all of this."

She sighed and set her tea cup down, fixing Abe with a stern glare. "If you are determined to marry this girl, then I know that nothing I say can change your mind, and I would little like to see my experience visited upon another generation. You have, I presume, already discussed the matter with her?"

Abe's head was spinning, both from the revelations about the strange and tragic link between his parents and Aunt Rosanna, and her sudden change of heart about his marriage to Betty. He managed to say weakly, "Aye, that we have."

She nodded crisply. "Then that settles the matter. You two can go to the blacksmith tomorrow, if you like, unless you should like to speak to the minister about giving you a ceremony."

"The . . . blacksmith?"

"Aye, he can witness a handfasting as well as anyone else, and where better to forge a union than over the anvil that he uses to forge iron?"

"I suppose," Abe said, hesitantly. To be honest, he had not thought so far ahead as to the actual ceremony that would be required to formalize his marriage to Betty.

Aunt Rosanna, though, took his hesitation to mean something different. "Are you unsure about marrying this girl so soon, then? If not now, why not wait a month, or even a year, to be sure that your proposal was not the result of a rash moment?"

Abe looked steadily at her. "Nay, 'Tis no such thing. I'll collect Betty in the morning, and we will see the blacksmith."

One of Aunt Rosanna's eyebrows rose in skepticism, but she said only, "Go and fetch your purse from the cabinet, then. I've no reason to hold it for you any longer, if you are so determined to make your own way in the world."

He rose to do as she said, his head still awhirl at how quickly she seemed to be changing her mind one way and then the other. She called after him, "You ought take a shilling out and split it with the axe; 'Tis traditional to give half at the close of the ceremony, and for husband and wife to each keep their half with them for so long as they live."

He stopped and looked at her. "For one who never married,

you know a great deal of the traditions and ceremonies that attend it."

"Of course I do, boy," she said tartly. "Just because I never got to marry my man doesn't mean that I haven't thought of it every night since we were parted."

Chapter 32

The sun shone warmly though the trees, and the air was sweet with the last of the springtime flowers. Abe and Betty sat side-by-side, their backs against one of the great mast trees in their grove. In the distance, Abe could hear the sounds of hammering and men calling back and forth as they worked on expanding and improving his old cabin.

Betty laughed at something, and he looked where she was pointing to see her raven hopping down from the branches overhead, a ribbon clutched in his beak. Abe sighed and put his arm around Betty. "I'll be glad when the roof is done," he said.

Betty laughed again and said, "I suppose I shall just have to leave my hair down tomorrow, then." She turned to face him, and he bent to kiss her.

He shrugged. "I like it better that way, anyhow." Looking up past the raven into the wide and spreading canopy of the trees overhead, he added, "Of course, you could always ask him nicely to return it." The raven cocked his head at Abe as though pondering his words, and then leapt into the air, flying out of sight through the boughs, trailing the ribbon behind.

Abe and Betty leaned into one another and started chortling together, the sound of their laughter rising into the cathedral of the trees like a birdsong.

Also in Audiobook

Many readers love the experience of turning the pages in a paper book such as the one you hold in your hands. Others enjoy hearing a skilled narrator tell them a story, bringing the words on the page to life.

Brief Candle Press has arranged to have *The Tree* produced as a high-quality audiobook, and you can listen to a sample and learn where to purchase it in that form by scanning the QR code below with your phone, tablet, or other device, or going to the Web address shown.

Happy listening!

bit.ly/TheTreeAudio

Historical Notes

First and foremost, a confession; I compressed the sequence of events between the seizure of the illegally-harvested timber from the mills and the riot considerably for the sake of my narrative. Historically, Governor Wentworth sent his surveyor—and even personally traveled around the state—to look for illicit timber during the winter of 1771-72; he did not actually issue charges until February of 1772.

That part, at least, fits the timeline as I've presented it. However, the betrayal of the mill owners by their lawyer, who accepted a post with the governor as an assistant surveyor—charitable interpretations say that it was offered so that he would better understand the difficulties against which the governor was working, rather than as a payoff to cause him to change sides—didn't take place until March of that year.

The sheriff did not issue a warrant for the arrest of the mill owners who refused to pay (or were unable to do so) until April of 1772, and the events I've depicted at the Pine Tree Tavern did not take place until then, so the snowstorm and its effects on the attack on the sheriff and his deputy are entirely inventions of my own.

Too, the Pine Tree Tavern stood in Weare, which is considerably further from Portsmouth than an afternoon's ride. Again, for the purposes of the story, I compressed the trip from the capitol to the scene of the riot.

The grisly details of the attack, however, were recorded quite credibly, and included in the warrants sworn out against the rioters. Regardless of our opinion of the ultimate justification for resistance to the King's demands on New England timber, it's worth remembering that mob violence was the form which a lot of the early action of the Revolution took.

Later, of course, the mobs were transformed into proper militias, and then into a regular Continental Army, and with assistance from England's other enemies, defeated the Crown's forces to permanently sever the bonds between Britain and her American colonies.

Acknowledgements

The process of writing historical fiction requires immersion into the world I'm writing about, and it's nearly impossible for me to enumerate the many sources I consulted in the process of writing *The Tree*.

I was fortunate in the preservation of first-hand accounts of a couple of pivotal moments in this book, and the fine work done by Google and their ongoing effort to digitize old sources was instrumental in locating those sources.

As usual, I'd like to acknowledge the substantial contributions of my editor at Green Ink Proofreading, whose many helpful suggestions and corrections improved this novel greatly. In addition, the wonderfully generous comments and suggestions from Hal Lane made this a far better-crafted story than it would otherwise have been. Discovering a shared love for observational astronomy in the course of our delightful discussions was a bonus. Any errors, of course, that persist into the final text remain entirely my own.

Thank You

I deeply appreciate you spending the past couple of hundred pages with the characters and events of a world long past, yet hopefully relevant today.

If you enjoyed this book, I'd also be grateful for a kind review on your favorite bookseller's Web site or social media outlet. Word of mouth is the best way to make me successful, so that I can bring you even more high-quality stories of bygone times.

I'd love to hear directly from you, too—feel free to reach out to me via my Facebook page, Twitter feed, or Web site and let me know what you liked, and what you would like me to work on more.

Again, thank you for reading, for telling your friends about this book, for giving it as a gift or dropping off a copy in your favorite classroom or library. With your support and encouragement, we'll find even more times and places to explore together.

larsdhhedbor.com
Facebook: Lars.D.H.Hedbor
@LarsDHHedbor on Twitter

Enjoy a preview of the next book in the
Tales From a Revolution series:

The Mine

A lec Tinsworth looked up, bidding the sun farewell. He didn't know how long it would be before he saw its light again, how long he would instead live by the flickering light of torches and candles—or less.

The man at the top of the mine shaft looked down at him without pity, and Alec returned his baleful glare, his feet questing one after the other for the next step on the unsteady ladder. At last, he came to a point where there was no next step, and the guard shouted down at him, "Just drop on down. It's not so far as you will fall into the hereafter."

A coarse bark of laughter echoed down the shaft to Alec's ears, and he lowered himself by his arms alone. He grimly felt for the floor that he expected to find, his foot describing wider and wider arcs through open air, until he lost his grip on the ladder and fell with a grunt into a jumbled pile of limbs. He rolled along the floor, which he was relieved to discover was strewn with straw. Without that, his fall might have done more than merely knocked his breath out for a moment.

As he lay catching his breath, he heard another guffaw from overhead, followed by the echoing boom of the door closing. The dim light that reached the bottom of the pit winked out, and Alec stayed very still, his eyes adjusting to the incredible darkness in which he now found himself.

As he waited for his eyes to find enough light to let him find his way deeper into the living quarters he'd been told to expect in the abandoned mine, he thought about the bitter road that had brought him here.

The light of the waning moon glinted through the bare branches of the woods, and Alec walked as silently as he could, desperately trying to find his way back to his patrol. He heard the snap of a twig stepped upon by a less cautious foot than his own, followed by a challenge in a low, urgent voice.

"King and country," the stranger called out, and Alec felt a wave of relief wash over him like the first splash of water in the morning from a springtime stream.

He answered, wearily, "King and country," and stepped out into a small clearing, where the wan light of the slender moon shone clearly on him.

The other voice called out more confidently now. "Got ourselves another Tory straggler, John." Alec felt a different sort of chill wash over him, and the stranger now addressed him, his tone not unkind, but firm. "If you be armed, you'd best drop down your weapon, good sir. We'll be delivering you up for parole if you be an officer, and for prisonment otherwise."

"I've no weapon save my knife," Alec called back resignedly. He raised his hands where anyone could see them in the moonlight, and the stranger stepped into the clearing with him, soon followed by his companion.

The one who had to be John stepped around behind Alec, his hands questing along his prisoner's waist, and up to his raised hand, which he pulled down behind Alec's back, reaching up to bring the other beside it. "Where's this knife, friend? I don't feel a belt or bag upon you."

"Nay, I've neither. 'Tis in my boot, this one." He slowly raised his left foot, balancing carefully on the right foot.

"Stand steady, Tory. I'll retrieve it while Jim binds your hands."

Jim's hands took the place of John's, and Alec could feel the rough texture of hempen rope being wrapped securely around his wrists, as John pushed his raised foot to the ground and reached into Alec's boot top to retrieve the knife.

John stepped back, and Alec could see him testing the blade's edge with his thumb in the half-light. Shaking his head in disappointment, John tossed the knife off into the darkness.

"Smart of you not to run or resist, Tory," Jim's voice sounded calm in Alec's ear. "John's not afraid to shoot into the darkness when he is confident that no friendly forces lie before us."

"That knife would have done you no good against any man, either," said John. "Have you a name, Tory?"

"Aye," Alec said glumly. "I am Alexander Tinsworth, of His Majesty's Loyal Connecticut Militia, a private soldier."

Jim asked, his voice astonished, "Alec? Why, your father and mine worked together in town, before the troubles started. I'm Jim Hudgins, and my old Pa was always suggesting that I'd do well to emulate your good example in all the things your father used to tell him about you."

He chuckled humorlessly to himself and added, "I don't suppose that my Pa would say quite the same now, though, if he were still with us to offer an opinion."

"I am sorry to hear that you've lost your father, Jim. My

dad spoke well of him, up until he turned traitor to the King."

Jim cuffed him across the face with the back of his hand, though without much conviction behind the blow. He said,, "'Tis not my father who is found traitor to his country tonight, Alec. You'll keep a civil tongue in your mouth while we bring you in, and the Captain will decide where what's to be done with you."

John had poked Alec in the ribs then, pointing toward the first blush of sunrise visible through the trees. "You'll walk in front, Alexander, just in case there are any of your allies about, waiting to spring a trap on travelers. Don't get any ideas about running, though. We know these woods as least as well as you, and our hands aren't bound, so you'd likely just wind up tripped or tackled for your trouble. Then I'd be obliged to hobble you, though it might slow us all up even more."

His shoulders slumped, and his cheek warm from where Jim had struck him, Alec trudged into the darkness in the direction indicated. Behind him, he could hear Jim and John speaking quietly, but could only make out an occasional snatch of their conversation.

"Real shame about that family," he heard, but he didn't know if they were talking about his family or some other that had suffered misfortune in this accursed war. His parents had most recently been turned out of the home where Alec had grown up, the home that his grandfather had built of straight timber felled from their own land.

It was forfeit to the self-styled Committee of Safety, claimed as the price to be paid by a notorious Loyalist family, they'd said. Alec's father had set his jaw in the way that he had when he was faced with things that could not be changed, but which were not bearable, and had gathered up the few things that the Committee's representatives permitted him. Alec's mother, though, had fallen to her knees before the leader of the squad, wailing and begging that their property be spared.

The man's face had started out resolute, and the longer Alec's mother carried on, the stormier his face became. Finally, he'd called out to Alec's father, who was still carrying armloads of his papers and clothing out to the dooryard for inspection. "Sir, please gain control of your wife, else we shall be forced to silence her on your behalf."

Alec's father had hurried to his wife's side and bent beside her as Alec looked on, helpless rage coursing through his body. He stroked her back and spoke soothingly into her ear, and she'd regained her composure sufficiently to stand and stagger over to where Alec stood.

"See to your mother," his father had said brusquely, and had turned away, going back to the task at hand. Alec had stood beside her, feeling her quake with silenced sobs as she clutched his arm, and had resolved in that moment to do whatever it took to ensure that she need never again suffer powerless grief.

Alec was yanked out of this reminiscence by John's question to Jim, "Think we'll find any more of these sorry fellows tonight?"

Jim's voice carried more clearly than John's in the morning air, and Alec could hear him say, "Nay, I think we've got enough to fill up the mine already, and work what may be left to work there."

Look for The Mine: Tales From a Revolution - Connecticut at your favorite booksellers.